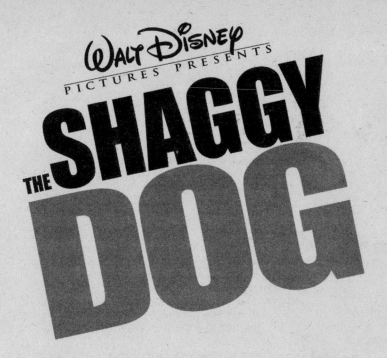

The Junior Novelization

Adapted by Gail Herman

Screenplay by The Wibberleys and Geoff Rodkey and Jack Amiel & Michael Begler

Based on "The Shaggy Dog" Screenplay by Bill Walsh and Lillie Hayward and "The Shaggy D.A." Screenplay by Don Tait

Produced by David Hoberman and Tim Allen

Directed by Brian Robbins

Disney
PRESS

D0172326

New York

First Edition
1 3 5 7 9 10 8 6 4 2

Library of Congress Catalog Card Number on file: 2005925553

ISBN 0-7868-4863-4
For more Disney Press fun, visit www.disneybooks.com
Visit DisneyChannel.com

PROLOGUE

Deep in the heart of The Himalayas, three men huddled around an old photograph. The men were soldiers of fortune, trained fighters who could be hired for any job.

The men stared at the photo. It was more than eighty years old, creased and curled around the edges. It showed other soldiers standing in front of a monastery. Behind them stood a big, shaggy sheepdog.

"This is your target," their leader declared. "He is to be captured, not harmed."

"Which man is it?" asked one soldier.

"We're after the canine," the leader answered. "His name is Khyi-yag-po. Translation: Dog of Ageless Wonder."

The men began to laugh, but stopped short when they saw their leader's serious face.

"You're crazy, man," the soldier said. "This picture is eighty years old. Everyone in that photo is dead."

The leader shook his head. "Not everyone . . ."

The monastery was nestled in the mountains, not far from the soldiers. Inside, a row of monks sat as still as statues, with their legs crossed. They chanted softly, seeking inner peace.

At the end of the row, in that same position, was Khyi-yag-po, the dog from the picture. "Araaoooo," he howled as if he were chanting.

A young boy poked his head through the door and smiled at the dog. Then he tossed a small ball outside. The dog scampered after it.

Khyi-yag-po chased the ball across a field and down a hill. He was almost there. He almost had it.

Suddenlly, a large boot stepped on the ball. Khyi-yag-po skidded to a stop and looked up. Three soldiers were staring at him. One drew a gun. He pulled the trigger, and an enormous net shot out. . . .

CHAPTER 1

Dave Douglas gazed at himself in the mirror. He straightened his tie and fussed with his hair. Today, he wanted everything to be perfect.

Dave was a high-powered lawyer—the assistant district attorney. And today was the start of his most important case ever. He was bringing Justin Forrester to trial.

All right, he thought, I'm almost ready. I just need to check the newspaper and see if the trial is on the front page. Dave smiled at his reflection. Then he practiced his speech as he walked to the front door. "... *teacher of children* ... too pompous? *A misguided young—*" Dave paused. "Dog?"

A small, wrinkled dog was about to go to the bathroom in Dave's front yard.

"Baxter!" Dave shouted to the dog's owner, his next-door neighbor. "Will you curb your mutt?"

Baxter stepped closer, chuckling. "Calling Attila a mutt is like calling my 2005 Porsche Carrera Turbo a '92 Buick Riviera."

"Whatever kind of car your dog is, stop old wrinkles here from peeing on my lawn," Dave replied.

"Your shrubs should be honored. He's seasoning them with his glorious tinkle. You hate dogs, don't you?"

"I don't hate dogs," Dave said. "I dislike dogs. I hate *your* dog." He grabbed the newspaper, then stormed inside.

In the kitchen, Dave's wife, Rebecca, was making lunch for their children to take to school. The local news played on a small TV. Dave opened the paper. "Will you look at this!" he cried. His case was the big news story! "Forrester's on the—"

He glanced at the TV. A man was being led out of a building in handcuffs. "Television? Come on!" Dave turned up the sound.

". . . the trial of Justin Forrester," the reporter was saying, "a local schoolteacher accused of arson in a fire at Grant and Strictland. Forrester denies the charges and claims the multinational has performed illegal genetic tests on animals. . . ."

Dave switched it off. "He's going down," he told Rebecca, picking up the newspaper again. "You can't burn a building because you think they're putting makeup on a bunny."

Of course, Forrester had thought the company did more than conduct makeup tests. Dave knew that. Forrester thought they were hurting animals. But still, starting fires? That was against the law— no matter what.

Rebecca sliced a sandwich. "You're going to Josh's parent-teacher conference. Right?"

"Right." Dave looked up from the paper. "What did you say?"

"Josh's parent-teacher thing," Rebecca repeated. "Four o'clock. You said you'd handle it."

Dave's eyes strayed back to the article. "Four o'clock, huh?" He had so much going on today. He wasn't sure he could make it. "What's your schedule like today?"

"I have a walk-through at three and a project meeting with the client and the architect at five," Rebecca answered.

"But nothing right at four?" Dave asked.

"I'm the only interior designer on this project," his wife replied. "And my teleportation machine's in the shop, so it might be hard for me to make it."

"I've got a trial starting," Dave said, "and Hollister's stepping down soon."

Didn't Rebecca realize how important this was, Dave thought. Ken Hollister, his boss, was about to retire. If Dave did a good job . . . if he won this trial . . . he could be the next district attorney. "Don't you want me to be the new DA?" he asked Rebecca.

Rebecca put down the knife. She was trying to stay calm. "Dave, you *never* go to these. Remember what the marriage counselor said about being more engaged in your children's lives?"

"She was totally looking at you when she said that," Dave said.

Rebecca glared at him.

"Kidding!" Dave cried. "I'll go to the meeting." He wrapped his arms around her waist. "Tell you what—when things settle down at work, what do you say we take that trip to AWWW WAHHH HOOO?"

"That way you say Oahu, that you think is so cute . . ." Rebecca began. "It only reminds me how many times you've canceled the trip."

Just then, Dave's twelve-year-old son, Josh, walked into the kitchen.

"Josh!" Dave said loudly and cheerfully. This

would show Rebecca. He *was* involved! "How's football going, killer?"

"Awesome!" Josh exclaimed, sounding even more cheerful than his father. "I'm playing tail-back!"

"Just like your old man. Fantastic. So when do I get to watch a game?"

"Oh," Josh shrugged and turned away. "They don't start for a while."

"I'm going by to see your teacher today. Any idea what she wants to talk about?" Dave asked.

"Probably just how much she likes me and how good I've been doing in every subject," Josh answered nervously.

Dave grinned at Rebecca. See how much he'd done already? And it was still breakfast! Dave took a sip of coffee. "Ugh!" He nearly spit it out. His daughter had just come into the kitchen. She was wearing a FREE JUSTIN FORRESTER T-shirt.

"Carly!" he cried. She's only sixteen years old, Dave thought. *I* should be her hero! Not her crazy teacher. "Take that shirt off!" he added.

"Why?" said Carly, just as angrily. "Did you drop the charges?"

Dave took a deep breath. "Sweetie, I know it's hard to believe. But your social studies teacher? The Torch? He's a criminal."

"What's hard to believe is that my father's defending a puppy murderer!" Carly countered. "Who are you going to put in jail next, Grandma?"

"Carly, the man set fire to their lab. Case closed," Dave responded.

"Except he says he's innocent," Carly said. "And I believe him."

Dave turned to his wife. "Will you help me out here?"

"Wear whatever you want, sweetie," Rebecca said with a smile.

"Thanks, Mom!" Carly said.

Beep, beep! A car horn sounded outside. It was Carly's boyfriend, Trey.

"That's Trey. Josh, want a ride?" Carly asked.

"In Trey's car?" Josh asked. "Yeah."

Without another word, the kids grabbed their backpacks and kissed their mother good-bye. As they walked out the door, Dave gasped. The back of Carly's shirt had his picture on it—with a slash right across the face.

"If I was putting your physics teacher in jail, you'd be thrilled!" Dave yelled after them.

Rebecca looked at her husband and walked toward the stairs to finish getting ready for work.

"How could you take her side?" Dave asked.

"Standing up for what she believes in? As a parent, that's kind of a no-brainer," Rebecca replied.

"She doesn't believe in it!" Dave protested. "She's just parroting back what her teacher told her!"

"I can't believe how clueless you are," Rebecca said, as she walked up the stairs.

"Yeah, well, neither can I," Dave said.

CHAPTER 2

Later that morning, Dave stood at the front of the courtroom. Every seat was taken—it was almost time for his opening statement.

Dave squared his shoulders. This was his moment to shine, to show the world he was ready to be district attorney. He faced the jury, the twelve people who would decide Forrester's fate. And maybe his own.

"Justin Forrester is a passionate advocate of animal rights," Dave began. "I respect that. But this case is not about animal rights. It's about whether the defendant criminally trespassed on Grant and Strictland Industries and set a fire that caused over $100,000 in property damage." He walked over to a display board with photos of a lab that had burned down.

In the courtroom, Dave's boss, Ken Hollister looked on intently. Beside him was Dr. Kozak, from Grant and Strictland. Kozak gave a slight smile, revealing sharp, fanglike teeth.

"Mr. Forrester," Dave went on, "admits to breaking in, but he claims the fire was set by Grant and Strictland employees to cover up a 'mysterious plot' involving 'harmful animal tests.'

"Folks," Dave continued, "not only is there *no* animal testing of *any* kind at the location he broke into, but this is a company dedicated to doing *good*—from its line of organic pet foods and animal shampoos to the lifesaving medications it's created to help people just like you and me fight heart disease, arthritis . . ."

An elderly juror looked interested.

". . . diabetes, obesity . . ." Dave went on.

An overweight juror raised his eyebrows.

". . . and yes, even baldness."

A bald man's eyes widened in excitement.

As Dave continued, Kozak grinned confidently at Hollister. There was no doubt about it. Dave Douglas was the best man for this job.

When court adjourned for the day, Dave stepped outside. Immediately, he was surrounded by news reporters.

"Think you can prove your case beyond a reasonable doubt?" one reporter asked.

"Well, Forrester went on your six o'clock news and bragged that he broke in the place, Will. By the way, I'll be subpoenaing that tape."

The reporters laughed. Good press was important, Dave knew, when you were running for the office of district attorney.

As the reporters dispersed, Dave's paralegal, Lori, handed him a piece of paper. "Here's your messages.

I'm holding four o'clock open for your kid."

"Yeah, right, four o'clock—" Dave stopped as his boss and Kozak walked toward them.

"Dave, great opening!" Hollister said. "You really won over that jury."

"You taught me everything I know, Ken," Dave said and shook his boss's hand. "Dr. Kozak, great to see you, sir," he continued. "Sorry we didn't have time to get you on the stand today."

"Apology accepted," Kozak replied. "Ken tells me after he steps down, you'll be our next district attorney."

"I sure hope so," Dave said. "But that's up to the voters to decide."

"Put this Forrester punk away," Kozak told him, "and you've got my support . . . and Grant and Strictland's. Until tomorrow, gentlemen."

As Kozak walked away, Hollister whispered to Dave. "Lance Strictland, Grant and Strictland's CEO, bankrolls a lot of campaigns. They could be a powerful ally."

* * *

Kozak drove straight to Grant and Strictland Industries. As he walked into the building, a man in a wheelchair rolled into the hallway. "Kozak!" the man called. "How'd it go in court today?"

"Ah, Mr. Strictland." Kozak stopped to talk to the company's owner. "It went very well, sir."

Gnarled and ancient, Strictland moved forward in his wheelchair. "I still don't understand why we're trying this case," he said.

"Let's talk in the elevator," Kozak said. "I have something to show you."

Strictland brightened. "Have you unlocked the dog's secret?"

The men got on the elevator. Kozak turned a key, and the elevator went down.

"We are trying this case because once Forrester saw what he saw, we had to be sure when he went public, he'd look like a mentally unbalanced criminal. After that, if we didn't press charges, we'd look like we were hiding something."

"I just hope it's worth hiding," Strictland said.

"It is," Kozak replied confidently. Just when the doors began to open, Kozak pressed the CLOSE button.

"What are you doing?" Strictland asked, surprised.

"I just want to make sure we're clear," Kozak answered in a low, menacing voice. "I'm getting the money and the credit this time. Right?"

"Of course."

"It's not going to be like the baldness cream?"

"No!" Strictland answered. "I'll take care of you this time. I promise."

"Good." Kozak lifted his finger. The doors opened. They entered a secret laboratory.

The room was crowded with computers, medical devices, and monitors. Animal cages holding rabbits, rats, and a monkey lined one wall. Another cage held Khyi-yag-po, the shaggy sheepdog from the monastery. All of the animals had wires hooked up to their bodies. The wires sent information flashing to computer screens.

But only the sheepdog was wired all the way from his nose to his tail.

Gwen and Larry, two lab workers, were busy taking notes on the animals.

"So, have you figured out why the dog has lived so long?" Strictland asked.

Kozak gave a half-nod. "You're familiar with the concept of dog years?"

"Don't like dogs," Strictland muttered. "I keep a squirrel."

"A pet squirrel? Huh." Kozak paused. "Dogs typically age seven years for every human year. But in this one, a genetic mutation reversed the equation. He lives seven years for every human year. This dog is over three hundred years old."

Strictland rolled his wheelchair forward. "The things you must have seen," he said to the dog.

"If we could transmit that gene to humans, we'd live for seven hundred years!" Kozak offered.

The lab assistants stopped their work. "We

discovered the gene fairly quickly," said Larry.

"But we were unable to viralize it outside his body for transmission to other species," Gwen added. "So we had to viralize his entire genetic code *in corpus*."

Strictland peered at the dog. He pointed to a drop of saliva hanging from the dog's tongue. "Which makes all his fluids . . ."

" . . . pretty dangerous stuff," finished Gwen. "But they'd have to enter the bloodstream to do any damage."

"We're very careful," Larry added.

Strictland looked at them. "So how close are we?" he asked.

The assistants wheeled a covered cage forward. They pulled off the blanket. Inside, an African cobra bared its fangs.

"When we got this snake, it was almost dead of old age." Kozak said. "Since we injected it with the serum made from the dog's viralized DNA, his cell degradation has ceased. And he's actually been getting stronger. It's quite remarkable. Three days ago he could barely move."

The snake hissed as he reached for a cricket that Gwen dropped in his cage. as it uncurled, they saw its entire body. Strictland gasped. "Does that snake have a furry tail?"

Kozak shrugged. "A minor side effect."

"Kozak," Strictland said sternly. "Dry mouth is a minor side effect. Growing a dog's tail turns your serum into a carnival act."

"We'll work it out. Don't worry, Lance—you and I will have the patent on the fountain of youth!" Just then, Kozak's cell phone rang. He answered it. "Yes? I'll be right there." He snapped his phone closed. "Excuse me," he said. "It seems we have a protest on the front lawn."

CHAPTER

3

Outside the offices of Grant and Strickland, protesters were lying flat on their backs, chanting, "Grant and Strictland's lying. So we're lying down!"

Police officers were watching the protesters. Kozak strode over to Dave who had just arrived. "When I called you, it was to make sure these people were arrested."

Dave waved to a television crew that was filming. "Trust me," he told Kozak. "If you arrest them, they wind up rebels with a cause on the six o'clock news. If you leave them alone, they're just kids lying on a sidewalk."

Kozak thought for a moment, and nodded. "Good advice. Thanks for the help." Then he turned to go back inside.

"Hi, Dad!" one of the protestors said.

Dave stopped. It couldn't be. Was that Carly lying on the ground? Dave backed up. It was. "Carly! What are you doing?" he demanded.

Carly squinted up at him. "Lying down for what I believe in."

"Good to see you, Mr. Douglas." Trey, Carly's boyfriend, was lying next to her.

"Hello, Trey," Dave said quickly. He looked at his daughter. "Can I speak to you for a moment?"

"Sure thing." She wriggled over a few inches. "Trey, make some room for Dad."

Dave leaned down. He pulled Carly up, then dragged her over to a quiet spot on the grass.

What is going on? he wondered. How could his daughter turn her back on her own father? "I want you out of here right now," he said with a hiss as Trey ambled up to them.

"I'm sorry." Carly brushed herself off. "But as a member of the Animal Rescue Group, there are certain principles—"

"You're not the member of a front. You're not a member of any movement." Dave interrupted. "You're a member of the eleventh grade. And if you don't go home, you're grounded."

"Who's going to enforce it, you?" Carly shot back. "You're never home."

"And you will never leave our home if you don't get out of here." Dave crossed his arms.

Carly spun on her heels. "Ugh. Come on, Trey!" she said indignantly.

Trey smiled awkwardly at Dave. "Good seeing you!"

Dave watched them walk away. That was one thing done. Now for the news reporters . . . "Hey, fellas! Slow news day, huh?"

While the protest continued outside, Larry and Gwen worked in the laboratory. Khyi-yag-po stood in front of them, on a table. Nearby, a frog with the head of a bulldog barked.

Larry jumped. "That one still freaks me out."

Gwen held a needle. "You can't make an omelet without breaking some eggs. Let's get a blood sample," she told Larry.

Larry held the sheepdog still. Gwen pushed the needle in. The dog didn't flinch or bark.

"Such a good boy. Never give us any trouble, do you—" Gwen cooed. She put the needle down.

Quick as lightning, Khyi-yag-po grabbed the needle in his mouth. He pointed it at Gwen. "Ahhh!" she shrieked, jumping back.

The sheepdog turned to Larry. "Grrrrr!"

Larry backed away. "Omigosh, it's a trap!"

"Dogs don't set traps," Gwen muttered.

"Dogs don't live three hundred years either!" Larry cried.

"Get the cattle prod," Gwen said, pointing to a

long electric pole she used to give the animals mild shocks.

Larry edged slowly to the cattle prod. He kept his eyes on the sheepdog. Khyi-yag-po kept the needle trained on Larry.

Ding! The elevator door opened, and Kozak stepped out. "Watch out!" Gwen called to him. "That blood's viral!"

The sheepdog leaped off the table and raced toward Kozak, who jumped clear as the dog bounded past him.

Khyi-yag-po ran right into the elevator, keeping the needle in his mouth until the door closed. He pressed the lobby button with his nose. The elevator rose. When the doors opened, Khyi-yag-po streaked down a hall.

At the same time, Carly and Trey were walking past the Grant and Strictland offices. "He treats me like a ten-year-old," Carly muttered. Suddenly, she stopped and gazed at the door to the loading dock. It was open and unguarded.

Trey followed her gaze. "What are you thinking?"

"That we can prove Mr. Forrester's right."

Trey looked at her incredulously. "You want to break in? I've got to be honest, I'm a little intimidated by you."

"Just follow me," Carly said confidently as she headed down an empty hallway.

"It's the middle of the day," Trey protested.

"And if anybody stops us," Carly said, "we're just looking for a bathroom."

Then, just as they turned a corner, the sheepdog barreled into them. For a moment, they stared at one another in stunned silence.

"Woof!" The sheepdog raced away, looking over his shoulder at the teenagers.

Carly and Trey followed. Here was an animal they could save! They raced out of the building into the parking lot. Carly and Trey jumped into their car. Khyi-yag-po sprang into the backseat.

"Go, go, go!" shouted Carly.

Trey sped away.

"We did it!" Carly exclaimed. "We proved Mr. Forrester's right. They *are* testing animals in there."

"Well, they do make dog food," Trey responded.

"Not in there they don't," Carly said.

"So now what do we do?" Trey asked.

"We'll take him to the media!" Carly said excitedly. "And show them that we've got this . . ." She slowed down. ". . . dog who's . . . got no tags or markings . . . that we . . . can't actually prove came from Grant and Strictland."

"Can we take him to your dad?" Trey asked a moment later.

"Oh, sure! And as the deputy DA, he'll arrest us for burglary."

Khyi-yag-po's ears pricked with interest.

"So what do we do with him?" Trey asked.

CHAPTER 4

A little while later, Rebecca came home to find a sheepdog playing tug-of-war with Josh in the backyard. "He's a stray?" Rebecca asked doubtfully.

"He was wandering the freeway," Carly explained. She tried to look truthful. "If we hadn't picked him up, he could've been killed."

Rebecca shook her head. "He looks awfully clean for a stray."

"We . . ." Carly thought quickly. ". . . gave him a bath. At Trey's house. Should've seen him—filthy! Clearly, this dog had no home."

The sheepdog pulled hard on the rope. Josh tumbled over, laughing. "Awesome!" he cried. "We should have gotten a dog a long time ago."

"Josh, we're not keeping him," Rebecca said. "Your father would never allow it. He hates dogs."

Carly smiled sweetly at her mother. "You know, Mom, I've been thinking. Shouldn't the decision about a household pet be made by the people who actually spend a lot of time in the household?"

Rebecca sighed. "Well, the lawyer doesn't fall far from the tree, does it?" She paused. "Whatever you do, don't name him."

Her kids looked at her guiltily.

"You didn't name him, did you?" Rebecca asked.

"Shaggy!" Josh called from the dinner table. "Come here!"

Rebecca took a deep breath. It was bad enough

the kids had named the dog. But now, they were feeding him from the table! "Don't feed Shaggy table scraps," she ordered.

"Hey, everybody!" Dave walked into the kitchen. "Sorry I'm late. Is my dinner—"

"In the microwave," Rebecca and the kids said in unison.

Dave heated up the food and poured a drink of water. "See the trial coverage on the news? Great clip of me on Channel Eight."

Everyone waited for Dave to notice the dog. But he was too busy thinking about the trial.

"So . . ." Now Rebecca sounded angry. "How was the parent-teacher conference?"

"Oh . . . oh!" said Dave. He'd never made it over to the school. "I am *so* sorry! I got a call from this guy at Grant and Strictland and just completely for—"

His eyes finally fell on the sheepdog.

"There's a dog!" he cried. "In our kitchen!"

A few moments later, Dave tried to pull

Khyi-yag-po outside. "This is a dog-free house-hold!" he shouted.

"Dad, stop oppressing Shaggy!" Carly cried.

Dave turned and glared at his wife. "You *named* him?"

"Not on purpose. It just sort of happened." Rebecca paused. "He's very cute. And smart. And—"

Dave sneezed. "Hypoallergenic?! Forget it," he said with a roar. "These things contribute nothing to a home except a huge mess, muddy footprints, and drool. We finally got you two out of that stage. I'm not going back."

He dragged the sheepdog to the doorstep. Suddenly, the dog stopped struggling. The dog had spied the recycling bin, with the newpaper on top. Forrester's picture was on the front page.

Khy-yag-po let go of Dave and ran to the bin. Dave fell on the floor and glared at the dog.

"That was an accident," Carly said. "He's really sweet if you just get to know him."

Khyi-yag-po pawed the paper. "Woof!" he barked at Dave, trying to get his attention.

It didn't work. "No, Carly. He is going right back to wherever he came from," Dave pronounced.

The sheepdog froze in panic, and a wild look came into his eyes. Dave reached out to grab him, but Khyi-yag-po sank his teeth into Dave's hand.

"Owwwww!" Dave yelled. Inside Dave's body, the cells had already started to change. Some of them grew tails and chased other cells around.

Instantly, the sheepdog tucked his tail between his legs. He gazed up at Dave with sad puppy-dog eyes and whined.

"You scared him. Look how sorry he is!" Carly exclaimed.

"Carly—" Dave began.

Khyi-yag-po licked Dave's hand.

"Hey, cut it out!" Dave yelled at the dog.

Khyi-yag-po whined some more, trying to tell Dave he was sorry. He rubbed up against Dave.

"Aww, he was kissing it better," Carly said. "What could be more sweet? So no hard feelings, right?"

Dave shook his head. It was no use. He'd already made up his mind. "I'm calling the pound."

A few minutes later, Dave watched as the animal control truck carrying the sheepdog.

"He tried to apologize," Josh protested.

"He licked me!" Dave snapped. "That's not an apology—he was just making sure I tasted good so he could take another bite!"

"If he doesn't have rabies can we take him back?" Carly pleaded.

Dave looked at Carly and Josh and stomped off into the house.

Rebecca put her arms around her children's shoulders. "I think that was a 'no.'"

CHAPTER 5

The Douglas home was finally quiet. Shaggy had been taken to an animal shelter, and Josh and Carly were in their rooms.

Dave was working in his office, surrounded by his high school football pictures. At his desk, Dave pored over some papers. His tongue lolled out of his mouth. "Hah, hah," he breathed loudly. It sounded like he was panting.

"How's your hand?" Rebecca asked, coming into the office.

Dave examined the bandaged bite. "Thine. Thankth."

Rebecca stared at him. "Why are you talking that way?"

Dave's tongue curled back into his mouth. "I don't know."

"Josh's teacher called me at work when you didn't show," Rebecca continued.

"I am *so* sorry—" Dave began.

Rebecca was tired of her husband's excuses. She interrupted. "He's flunking math."

Dave sat back. "You're kidding me! Well, he knows he can't play football if he doesn't keep his grades up. I'll talk to him, don't worry." Then he went back to work.

"She also asked if there was anything wrong at home," Rebecca said.

"Mmm-hmm," Dave answered, still engrossed in his reading.

Rebecca stared at him. "I told her we'd resorted to cannibalism and were eating our neighbors."

"All right," Dave said without looking up.

Rebecca stood a moment and stared at her husband. She picked up a stack of heavy law books and raised them over her head, waiting for him to notice. But it was no use. She dropped the books, which landed with a loud crash on the floor.

Dave jumped.

"Where did my husband go?" Rebecca asked angrily. "The guy who once spent a month helping Carly build a diorama can't even make a parent-teacher conference?"

"Don't exaggerate the problem," Dave said.

"Dave, what does it tell you that you were bitten by a stray dog—and your kids took the dog's side?"

Dave tried to convince her she was wrong. "You know, as fathers go, I'm pretty plugged in."

"Really?" Rebecca said. "Did I tell you when I picked up Josh from football last week, one of his coaches asked me out?"

"Seriously?"

"Seriously," Rebecca confirmed. "He'd somehow gotten the idea I was a single mom."

"Wow," Dave said. "Okay, I'm going to start going

to football practice. And could you never go again?"

"And," she rushed on, "forgetting the fact that I'm in the middle of the biggest interior of my career, and am getting absolutely no support at home. When's the last time you even remembered to say, 'I love you'?"

"I love you!" Dave cried out quickly.

"No, see that one doesn't count," Rebecca said.

Dave tried to look deep into her eyes. "Tell you what—I'll come home early tomorrow. Cook dinner for the kids, spend some quality time. And you know what the next night is?"

"Do you?" Rebecca challenged.

"It's our anniversary! We'll go to dinner. I'll sing to you in my lousy French accent. Insist that you order the chocolate soufflé, which you will not regret. What do you say?"

Rebecca shook her head. "You can't just talk a good game. You've got to follow through. If you don't plug back into this family . . . we've got problems counseling can't fix."

"Heeeyyy," Dave said softly.

She looked at him seriously.

"Let's not go there. I love you!" Dave said again. "Okay?" He looked at his wife tenderly, but he felt distracted. Something itched behind his ear. He scratched it. That felt so good! He scratched a little more. Then even more.

"You all right?" Rebecca gave him a funny look.

"Yeah!" Dave kept scratching and scratching. "Just a . . . little itch."

Dave woke up early the next morning. He was curled in a ball at the foot of his bed. That was odd. But he'd slept great. He'd had this dream that he was chasing a car.

"Rough night's sleep?" Rebecca asked.

"No, I slept great," he replied.

Dave stretched, sticking his behind in the air, just like a dog.

Rebecca gazed at him strangely and went into the bathroom.

"Had the weirdest dream, though," Dave called. "I was chasing this car. . . ." He put on a bathrobe, but the belt was tied behind at the back.

"Hey!" Dave told his wife. "Let's go someplace today. Let's go outside! Run around the park, roll in the grass! Just outside somewhere." He spun around in a circle chasing his bathrobe tie like a dog would chase its tail.

"Don't you have to be in court?" Rebecca called.

Dave whimpered. He really wanted to play in the park. But he did need to go to work. Once Rebecca was done, he hopped into the shower. When he got out, he shook himself dry. Who needed a towel? He dressed carelessly. What difference did it make if he combed his hair? He was planning to stick his head out the car window.

Suddenly, his ears quivered. Loud music was coming from Josh's room. It was a song from *Grease*. Dave raced down the hall and flung open Josh's door.

Josh wore a leather jacket over his football jersey. He was wearing headphones, and dancing and singing quietly.

"Turn that down!" Dave roared.

Josh took off the headphones, embarrassed to be caught singing. "Dad. Don't you knock?"

"I did. I could hear the music all the way in the bedroom. . . ." Dave said as he left the room.

But how? Josh wondered. He'd been wearing headphones.

Dave walked into the kitchen and smiled at Rebecca. Then he sniffed the air. "Bacon! Love the smell of bacon! But there's something else, too. Is that hibiscus? And cedar?"

"That's my perfume!" Rebecca said in surprise. She sniffed her wrists. "Did I put too much on?"

"No, it's nice," Dave said. He noticed that classical music was playing. "How come you're listening to music?"

"You mean . . . like I do every morning?"

"Those high notes are so intense," he said.

Rebecca was staring at him. He smiled and kissed her. "Great music, great smells, a beautiful wife— wow! My kitchen's a paradise!"

Dave poured a cup of coffee. He stuck his nose in the mug and lapped it up. He made a face. "Coffee's kinda strong." He took a plate of bacon instead. "Josh!" he cried, seeing his son sit down. "Mom says your math grade's down."

Josh nodded. "Yeah, it's been really hard this year. I guess I should—"

He paused. His father was snapping up bacon with his teeth.

"—spend more time studying," Josh finished slowly.

"Are we going to have to pull you out of football?" Dave reminded him.

"Dad!" Josh sounded upset. "You wouldn't do that. Would you?"

"Hey, I want you out there playing as badly as you do. But if you can't keep your grades up, you can't play football." He grabbed more bacon with his teeth and looked at his watch. "Oooh, gotta run." Then he hugged Rebecca. "I love you. Does that count?"

"I don't know. Maybe," she replied.

Dave grinned. He leaned forward to kiss his wife. Instead, he licked her cheek. "Bye," he said and raced out of the house.

Rebecca and Josh looked at each other. Then they looked at the open door. "He's been working very hard lately," Rebecca told Josh. She hoped that explained her husband's strange behavior.

Outside, Dave noticed that Baxter's dog, Attila, was about to go to the bathroom in his yard— again.

"Hey!" Dave yelled. "This is my yard! My yard! MY YARD! Nobody pees here but me!"

"Morning, Baxter," Dave said and drove off sheepishly.

Baxter looked down at his dog. "Don't you worry, champ. You just keep peeing on the bad man's lawn."

CHAPTER

6

It was the second day of the Forrester trial. Kozak was on the stand, telling his side of the story.

"Security called me in the middle of the night. That's when I discovered the fire. Fortunately, the sprinklers put it out before it spread to the rest of the building."

"Dr. Kozak," Dave said. "I have some papers I'd like you to look at."

He picked up the papers with his teeth. Then he loped over to Kozak and thrust them out. Kozak reached for them. Dave pulled back, teasingly. It was like a playful tug-of-war.

Finally, Kozak grabbed hold of the papers. Dave unclenched his teeth. The game was over. "Can you tell me what that is?" he asked Kozak.

"It's the company's policy on animal testing. We perform only humane, noninvasive tests. And I should add that none of it takes place in the building where the fire—"

Forrester's lawyer interrupted. "Objection, Your Honor!"

Dave whirled to face her. He bared his teeth and growled.

"Mr. Douglas!" the judge exclaimed. "Did you just growl at opposing counsel?"

"Of course not, Your Honor!" Dave said quickly. "I just have . . . a tickle in my throat. Probably my allergies. Aaaah-choo!" He pretended to sneeze.

"Do you need to take a short recess?" the judge asked.

"No, thank you. Can we RRRR—" Dave clapped a hand over his mouth.

"Did you just growl at *me*?" the judge demanded.

"No! I have something in my thRRRRRRR—"

Dave strode to a table and gulped down a drink of water. "Okay," he said. "RRRRRRR!"

A few people laughed.

"One more outburst, Mr. Douglas, and I'm holding you in contempt," the judge said sternly.

Terrified, Dave whispered, "Can I have that, um . . RR. RRRR . . ."

"Rrrecess?" the judge asked.

"Yes!" Dave cried.

The judge banged her gavel. "Ten minutes!"

In the men's room, Dave tried to get it together. "Calm down, just calm down," he told himself. "Deep BRRR. BRRRR. Inhale. Okay." He breathed deeply. Then he raised his leg to go to the bathroom.

No! Dave thought. What was happening to him? He looked down at the bite on his wrist. He scratched it gently. He sniffed. Then he licked it. "Ew!" he said in disgust. But he licked it again.

"Ewww!" And again. He raced out of the bathroom.

"Lori, sick!" he panted to his assistant, who was waiting outside. "Leaving. Tell judge."

He raced past a waiting group of reporters. "Hey, Dave!" one called. But Dave kept running, not looking back.

A few minutes later, Dave was talking with the employee at the animal shelter Shaggy had been brought to.

"He definitely doesn't have rabies," the employee said.

"Then what does he have?" Dave demanded.

"Silky coat, great disposition—I tell you, that is one good dog."

There had to be something wrong with the dog. "Where is he?" Dave asked.

The shelter worker directed Dave to a row of cages. Dogs barked at him as he passed. "Grrrrrr!" Dave growled back.

Why did he keep growling? What was wrong with him?

Thump, thump. Dave's heart raced. Finally, he came to the cage that held Shaggy. The sheepdog sat calmly in his cage, almost like he'd been expecting Dave.

Dave looked at his dog bite, then at the dog. "What did you to me? Why am I acting like this?"

A small dog yipped next to Dave. Dave wheeled around. "Stop it!" he yelled.

A big dog lunged against his cage, growling.

Dave's heart beat even faster. He could feel it pounding inside his chest.

The sheepdog reared up on his hind legs. He put his paws against the cage. "Woof, woof!"

Dave slammed his hands on the cage. He glared down. "Starp it!" he said. His voice sounded funny. Almost like a bark. "Rarp rit. Rrrrrrrr!" He could only growl now.

Inside Dave, dog cells raced around helter-skelter, taking over every inch of his body.

Boom, boom, boom. Dave's heart roared like a locomotive.

"How did you get so tall?" Dave said to the sheepdog. At least, that's what he tried to say. But all that came out was, "Woof, woof, ruff."

"Arf, arf," the sheepdog barked.

"Who's a dog?" Dave asked, confused. "Who said that?" He looked around, lost his balance, and landed on all fours. "Whoa, what happened there?"

Silence fell. The other dogs just stared.

Just then the animal-shelter worker came down the row. "How did you get out?" he said to Dave. He reached for a long stick with a loop of rope at the end. The control stick.

"Out?" Dave repeated. "What do you mean?"

"Arf!" said the sheepdog.

"Watch out for what?" Dave asked. Then he realized he had understood what the dog had been barking. "Was that you? How can a dog be talking to me?"

The worker swung the control stick. Dave jumped away just in time. "Hey!" What was going on?

The worker raised the stick again.

Dave didn't wait for any answers. He sprinted past the worker, out the door, and onto the street. His tongue flopped up and down.

"What is that?" he said. "Something is hitting me in the face." Then he realized. "Ugh! It's my tongue! I can taste my eyeball!"

Dave looked down at the sidewalk as he ran. "Those aren't hands! And why am I running on all fours? And why is running on all fours so much fun?"

He screeched to a stop in front of an electronics store. A big window display showed dozens of TV sets hooked up to a video camera. The camera was taping people walking past, and the TVs showed them on-screen.

Dave stared at the screens. Two dozen sheepdogs stared back at him. Was Shaggy here? he wondered. Dave raised one leg. So did the dog.

Dave gasped. "Is that . . . me? No. It's impossible. Am I inside a dog? Was I eaten by a dog? Did someone knock me out and put me in a dog costume?"

He shook his head. So did the TV dogs.

"It's a dream—gotta be. I'm asleep. Just have to wake up."

He ran headfirst into the store window. "Owwww!" he howled. If he had been sleeping, that would definitely have woken him up. He looked at the screen.

A big, shaggy sheepdog looked back.

"Okay. I'm not dreaming. So that means . . . *I'm a dog!*"

Meanwhile, Gwen and Larry were busy looking for Khyi-yag-po. They arrived at the animal shelter and noticed the worker standing at the door, looking for the sheepdog who had just left.

"Hi, there!" Larry said. "Hoping you can help us. Our dog wandered off. . . ."

CHAPTER 7

Dave raced down streets and highways. He had to get home and find Rebecca.

"Please be home," he panted. "Please be home."

Finally, there it was—the Douglas family house. Dave bounded up to the door and stood on his back legs trying to open it.

Useless paws, he thought. They don't work at all. He couldn't even ring the doorbell.

Finally, he pressed the button with his nose.

Carly opened the door. "Shaggy!" she cried happily. "You're back."

"I'm not Shaggy!" Dave tried to speak. But all that came out were arfs and woofs. "I'm Dad!" he barked. "You've got to help me, Carly. Somehow—it must have been the dog bite—I turned into Shaggy! Get Mom on the phone. We'll—"

Carly patted him. "Well, aren't you talkative?"

"Are you listening to me?" Dave barked.

Carly scratched his neck. "Carly, cut it—Ohhh! That feels good. Under the ear. No!" Dave shook his head. "Stop! Stop! Why don't you listen?" Then he realized why she wasn't listening. "Wait a minute. . . . So when I talk, all you hear is 'bark'?

"Great!" he said with a sigh. "All I can do is bark. That's just great." Carly scratched his throat. "Oooh, yeah. Right there."

"Hey!" Josh said , as he walked in the front door. "It's Shaggy. Where'd he come from?"

"Dad must have dropped him off," Carly said.

"No!" Dave barked. "Listen to me. *I'm* Dad. I'm your dad! I'M . . . YOUR . . . DAD!"

"Wow, he's really hyper today," Josh said.

Carly squatted beside Dave. "Do you need to do some business?" she said, like she was talking to a baby.

"No!" Dave barked, and barreled past his children. He had to make them understand.

In the living room, he scrambled around among the games and books. Finally he found what he was looking for. "Scrabble!" he cried.

He pushed the game to the floor. The box opened, and letters spilled out. He moved tiles here and there with his paw, searching.

"Shaggy! Bad doggy!" Carly scolded, as she entered the living room.

"Look at this!" Dave tried to say. "*I* . . ." Carly and Josh began to clear away the tiles, cleaning up. "Don't pick those up. *A* . . . *M* . . . Need a *D*. Quit cleaning up."

Carly scooped up the I, A, M, and D tiles, right under Dave's wet nose.

"Sixteen years, not once do you clean your room. And now this?" Dave barked.

Carly closed the box and put the game away.

Just then, a car horn beeped outside.

"That's Janey," Carly said. "I gotta go."

"Where are you going?" Josh asked.

"Promise you won't tell Mom and Dad?"

"I don't like the sound of this," Dave barked.

"I'm getting a tattoo!" Carly announced.

"*What?*" Dave barked and sprinted out the door toward Janey's car.

"Hey, Carly!" Janey called. "Hurry." She spotted Dave. "Oh, look, a doggy. *Aaahh!*"

She screamed and rolled up the window as Dave slammed into the door, snarling and barking.

"Janey, how could you?" Dave barked. "You were a good girl. You went to church camp."

Carly and Josh ran out the door toward the car. "Shaggy, stop it!" Carly ordered as Janey drove away. "What has gotten into you? Bad dog!"

"Don't use that tone of voice with me! You are grounded, young lady!" Dave cried.

As Dave barked, Carly started to back away from him. "He's kind of freaking me out," she said to her brother. "Maybe he should go back to the pound."

"Nooo!" Dave barked. "I'll be good—look!" He rolled around on his back. "I'm a good doggy! Look who's a good doggy. Wow, is this humiliating."

"He probably needs to run around a little," Josh suggested.

"I just ran five miles to get here!" Dave barked.

"I know. I'll take him to the dog park."

"We are not going to the dog park," Dave barked.

Minutes later, Dave was at the dog park.

"Shaggy!" Josh called. "Catch the Frisbee!"

Dave shook his furry head. "I am not catching any Frisbee!" Since he was there, he planned to talk to the other dogs. Maybe they'd heard of this human-turned-dog thing happening before. "I need to get some information from—"

Josh threw the Frisbee high into the air.

"I got it!" Dave couldn't help himself. He leaped after the disc, catching it in his mouth. "Yes, I nailed that!"

Just then a girl named Tracy rushed over. "Josh!" she said, upset.

"Oh, hey, Tracy. How's it going?"

"Where were you today?" she asked

"What do you mean?" Josh asked innocently.

"Auditions? For *Grease*? We were supposed to sing together," Tracy said.

Dave trotted up to Josh, holding the Frisbee in his mouth. "That instinct is really intense," he barked. He dropped the Frisbee at Josh's feet. "Here, keep the Frisbee. I gotta go talk to these dogs and find out—"

Josh tossed the Frisbee again. Dave bolted after it. "Mine!" he cried.

Josh turned to Tracy and tried to change the subject. "Got a dog. Pretty cool, huh?"

"Where were you?" Tracy repeated.

"Oh," Josh muttered. "I'm, uh, not doing the musical this fall."

"What?" she asked.

Dave brought the Frisbee back. "I don't have time for this!" he growled. "I've got a very serious—okay, one more." Josh threw it again.

Josh looked at Tracy. "I just, you know, don't want to."

Tracy glared. Then she began to laugh. She thought he was kidding! "Funny. You're cute. Be at the theater tomorrow. Three o'clock." She hit Josh in the arm in a friendly way. "And don't get cocky—you know Miss Loudon. Just 'cause you're the best doesn't mean you'll get the part."

She ran off. "Who's the girl?" Dave barked, loping back. "Why's she mad at you? Please don't throw that again." Josh threw it.

"Aagh!" Dave took off after it.

When Josh took Dave home, Rebecca and Carly

were sitting at the kitchen table. They both looked mad.

Dave bounded in. "Honey!" he barked. "Thank goodness you're home. Uh-oh. That's your mad face."

"What's for dinner?" Josh asked.

"Your father's cooking. At least, he was—the last time he returned one of my phone calls."

"Did you check your e-mail?" Carly asked.

"That's it!" Dave said to himself. "The computer!" He raced into his office and sat down at the desk. Then he picked up a pencil with his teeth and used it to peck at the keyboard.

```
Can't make dinner because I turned
into a dog. Am typing this with a
pencil in my teeth . . .
```

"Shaggy!" Carly cried as she and Josh walked into the office. "Stop causing trouble."

She turned off the computer without seeing the words. Dave looked around frantically. He needed something . . . something that would help his family realize who he was. Glasses!

He picked up his eyeglasses and flipped them onto his nose. "Look! Who does this remind you of?"

"Wow!" Josh exclaimed with a grin. "Maybe he escaped from the circus."

"Or maybe," Dave barked, "I'm your father!"

Just then Rebecca came into the office. "Rebecca!" Dave padded closer to her. "Honey! You recognize me. Don't you?"

Rebecca looked at Dave for a long moment. She searched his eyes. He thought she understood. Then she said, "Cute," and plucked off his glasses.

"So," Rebecca said to Carly and Josh. "Think your father will come through? Or should we order in?"

"Let's order in," they said together.

"Ouch!" Dave slumped. His family didn't expect him to keep a promise. That hurt.

Soon, the Chinese food arrived. "Omigosh,

that smells amazing. I'm swimming in the aroma of spring rolls. Can I please have some? Please, please, please?" Dave begged.

Rebecca shoved him away from the table and toward the bowl of dog food. "No," she said. "No people food for you."

"What? Dog food? No way. I don't want this. I want what people eat. I want people food." He stared at his bowl. "Oh, man. This is so unfair." He took a bite. "Ugh. I can't believe they call this chicken and gravy." He took another bite. "This is definitely not chicken. It's not gravy, either. What is that taste? Oh, man! I think it's horse." He took another bite. "And it's delicious."

After dinner, Rebecca, Carly, and Josh sang along to music, dancing and having a great time. Dave watched from the corner. So this is what I've been missing, he thought. That looks like so much fun. I didn't even know we still had karaoke night.

A new song came on, and Rebecca's smile

disappeared. It was a song she and Dave always sang as a duet. "I need your father for that one," she said.

"Sorry, honey," Dave barked. "It's been a while, hasn't it?"

Everyone sat down glumly. "Hey, come on!" Rebecca said, trying to stick up for Dave. "It's not so bad—he's working hard for us! And we get to see him on the TV. That's almost like being here. Kind of."

Dave sat up. "Honey, I am here!" he tried to say. "I'm your husband, Dave!" But all that came out was, "Rar, rar, ruff-ruff!"

Rebecca stared at the shaggy dog. "You know? I think he's trying to tell us something."

Dave ran in circles. She knew who he was! he hoped. "Yes, finally!"

"Carly," Rebecca went on, "take him out to do his business."

"What?" Dave barked.

Carly watched Dave run around outside.

Khyi-yag-po chanted with the monks.

"He lives seven years for every human year. This dog is over 300 years old," Kozak explained.

Dave and his family waited outside as Shaggy was
loaded into the animal control truck.

Dave grinned and leaned forward to kiss Rebecca.
Instead, he licked her cheek.

Kozak reached for the file in Dave's teeth,
but Dave pulled back.

Dave used the letter tiles to spell I AM DAD,
but Carly and Josh didn't understand.

Dave used a pencil to type on the keyboard.

Dave chased the cat in the alley.

After the football game, Dave followed Josh home.

Dave scurried down the street with a bouquet of roses in his mouth.

Trey, Carly, and Josh rescued Khyi-yag-po from
Grant and Strictland, thinking it was their dad.

Dave talked to his wife as he drove to court
with the animals from the lab.

Dave's family and Khyi-yag-po were waiting
for him outside the courthouse.

Dave edged closer and snarled at Kozak, who growled back.

A long, shaggy tail wagged at the base of Kozak's spine.

"So," Dave said to his wife and kids, "what do you say we take that vacation to AWWW WAHHH HOOO!"

"Shaggy, we're not going back inside till you leave me a little present," Carly said.

"This is a truly special moment in the father-daughter relationship. . . . Just let me find a good place." He slunk behind a tree.

That night, Rebecca led Dave into the garage. "Sorry, Shaggy," she told him. "I'd let you sleep inside. But my husband wouldn't allow it."

Dave sighed. "Now there's a bitter irony."

"Good night, Shaggy."

Dave barked. "Wait, honey."

Rebecca turned to look at him.

"I'm sorry about tonight. I love you. Aarr ruff roo."

"Sweet dreams, Shaggy," she said on her way out.

Later that night, moonlight streamed in through the garage window. As Dave slept, his heartbeat slowed. *Thump . . . thump.* And slowed some more. *Thump . . . thump.* When Dave woke up hours later, he was a human being again. Not a sheepdog.

Dave leaped up. Then he wrapped himself in an old blanket, and went to find his wife.

In the bedroom, Rebecca looked at him angrily. "It's 3:00 A.M.," she said. "Where have you been? And why are you wearing a blanket? And why aren't you wearing a wedding ring?"

"I know you're mad. And I would be, too. But there's a simple—although kind of hard to swallow—explanation." Dave gulped. "I . . . turned into a dog."

The next thing Dave knew, he was standing outside the bedroom, and the door had been slammed in his face.

CHAPTER

The next morning, Dave woke up as Carly walked by the couch.

"Wow. Somebody's in the doghouse," she said.

"Carly, where did you find Shaggy?" Dave asked.

"I told you, walking on the side of the freeway, by the mall," she replied.

"Just wandering along?"

"Yeah. When I see a stray, as a member of the Animal Rescue Group—"

Dave interrupted his daughter. "Oh, speaking

of which—if you want to put your beliefs in writing, try a letter to the editor. Not a tattoo."

"How did you . . . ?" Carly turned and ran the other way. "Josh, I'm going to kill you!"

Dave looked at the clock. He had to get going.

A few minutes later, he was at the doctor's office, telling his story. "Then I wake up, and I'm human again. So . . . what do you think?"

"Well, it's difficult to be sure. But if I had to guess, I'd say . . . *cuckoo!*"

"Seriously, Dave, even if that dog was rabid, you still wouldn't have these symptoms. You're clearly overworked. And this is your body's way of telling you to slow down, relax, and have a Milk-Bone."

Dave stared at the doctor, annoyed by his joke.

"Sorry. Look, try to take some time off. Catch up on your sleep, get some exercise, maybe chase a car." He paused. "I can't help it. It's too easy."

Dave hopped off the exam table. "Thanks for the help, Doc. Good luck with the nightclub act."

Dave needed to talk to Shaggy. So he drove to the animal shelter.

But Shaggy was gone.

Dave rushed over to the guy at the front desk. "Let me get this straight. You're telling me the dog was picked up by a Johnny Johnson of John Street?

"That's what the record says," the worker said.

"Didn't you ask for an ID?"

"We generally work on the honor system. Stray dog fraud just isn't a real huge problem for us," the guy countered.

Dave growled at him and stormed out.

A few minutes later, Dave arrived at work. "The parent-teacher conference got re-scheduled for noon," his assistant reminded him. "Anything else you need from me this morning?"

"I need some research," Dave said.

"On?" Lori asked.

"Dogs. And men. And men who . . . Have you ever heard of a man turning into a dog?"

She began to write. "Dogs, men, dog-men. I'm on it. But do you mind if I ask why you're looking into this man-dog . . . topic?"

"Be better if you didn't," Dave replied.

"Okay," Lori said.

Just then Hollister stepped into Dave's office.

"How are you feeling today, Dave?" Hollister asked him.

"Great," Dave said. "Just on my way to court."

"I'll walk with you," Hollister offered.

"Super," Dave said.

Hollister walked Dave to the elevator. "I'll be honest," he told Dave. "The reports of your behavior in court were unsettling. As was your disappearing the rest of the day."

"I know. I'm sorry," Dave said. "I had . . . some kind of food poisoning! I was mildly delirious."

The two men stepped into the elevator. "Wait!" a police officer called as he hurried in, holding a German shepherd by the leash.

"Why don't we take the stairs—" Dave began.

But the doors closed. The German shepherd sniffed Dave curiously.

"But, you're fine now," Hollister went on.

Dave nodded. "Absolutely! A hundred percent." He tried to step away from the German shepherd. But the dog strained on his leash. He kept sniffing. Dave's heart began to thump.

"Good. Because people don't want a loose cannon in the DA's office."

The dog was still sniffing. Dave's nose started to twitch and his lip curled into a snarl.

"By the way," said Hollister, "Lloyd Gannon called about working up some preliminary campaign ideas."

Dave looked at the officer, hoping he'd control his dog.

"Sit!" the police officer ordered.

The dog obeyed. So did Dave.

"He wants to go grassroots to start . . . mailers, door hangers . . . and work up to TV and radio," Hollister continued.

Instantly, Dave sprang back up. "Are you okay?" Hollister asked.

"Surrrrr," Dave answered, trying not to growl. He clamped his jaws tight and waited a moment. Nothing happened.

Dave relaxed. His tongue lolled out like a dog's. Horrified, he sucked it back in.

Finally the elevator doors opened. Safe, Dave thought, as he turned out.

"Are you sure you're good to go in court today?" Hollister asked.

Dave gulped, and tried to smile. "Oh, yeah," he told Hollister. "Fine."

In the courtroom, Dave faced Forrester once again. "I admit I broke in," Forrester explained. "But I swear I didn't set that fire. If you ask me, Dr. Kozak set it himself. He's trying to cover up what he's doing in that lab."

Dave leaned in closer. "Which, according to his testimony, is 'nothing.'"

"He's lying!" Forrester exclaimed. "I saw a dog hooked up to a horrible machine. He was full of needles. He looked so sad, tired. It was as if they were sapping the life out of him."

Dave glanced at the jury. They were listening to Forrester. Some shook their heads in sympathy. The jurors were on Forrester's side now. And Dave wanted them on his.

"The police didn't find any animals," Dave said.

"Then they moved them. There were poor little bunnies, fluffy bunnies together in a cage—"

"And you thought it was a good idea to set a fire where there were fluffy bunnies present?" Dave asked.

"Objection, Your Honor," Forrester's lawyer said.

"Overruled," the judge said.

"I didn't set it. I saw what I saw!" Forrester cried.

"Then why can't *we* see it, Mr. Forrester? Do we need special goggles? Was it a bigfoot kind of deal—" Dave demanded.

"Objection!" Forrester's lawyer shouted.

"Where the animals ran into the woods before anyone else—" Dave continued, talking over Mr. Forrester's attorney.

"I saw a monkey act like a dog!" Forrester blurted out.

Dave stopped short. His eyes widened. Another kind of animal . . . acting like a dog? Just like him!

The audience and the jury murmured and giggled. Now they were laughing at Justin Forrester. The judge banged her gavel. "Order," she called. "Counselors, please approach the bench."

As Dave and Forrester's lawyer walked toward the bench, Dave pushed her away from the judge.

"Are you herding me?" she asked Dave.

Dave realized that he was and backed away. When they got to the judge's bench, Dave rested his chin on it and looked at the judge with puppy-dog eyes.

"Mr. Douglas, get your chin off my desk," the judge ordered.

"Sorry," Dave said.

"I assume you're going somewhere with this that doesn't involve turning my courtroom into a barnyard again," the judge said.

"Absolutely, Your Honor. Yes I am." Dave raised his shirt quickly, flashing his belly in a sign of canine respect.

The judge looked confused. She turned to the witness. "Mr. Forrester, I suggest you limit your responses to the questions asked. Proceed, counsel."

Dave thought for a moment. "Let's stay with the monkey for a minute," he said. "How did it act like a dog?"

Hollister watched curiously. Where was Dave taking this? The judge watched closely, too. Kozak was also in court, his eyebrows furrowed with concern.

"It was growling. Chasing its tail."

The audience in the courtroom began to laugh.

"And the bunnies—anything out of the ordinary with them?" Dave asked.

"They were fighting over a dog toy, just like puppies," Forrester responded.

"Anything else biologically weird?" Dave asked.

"A snake with a tail like a dog. And rats that barked at me!"

The courtroom erupted in laughter. The judge banged her gavel, but it was no use.

"It's true. I'm not crazy," Forrester insisted. But no one was listening.

Dave glanced over at Kozak, who looked furious. But then Kozak noticed everyone else was laughing and tried to pretend to laugh, too. But Dave knew something wasn't right.

"The dog you saw," Dave whispered amid the laughter. "What did it look like?"

"It was a big, woolly sheepdog," Forrester explained.

Dave stared at him for a moment. "No further questions, Your Honor."

"Thank goodness," the judge replied.

Hollister looked on, pleased. Then Dave circled his chair three times, sniffed it, and pawed at it before he sat down. Hollister looked baffled by Dave's actions.

"Your witness, counsel," the judge announced. "Good luck."

"Your Honor, in light of . . ." Forrester's lawyer began. She paused. "Can I have a recess? Please?"

"Fine. Court adjourned," the judge said. Everyone cleared the courtroom.

Dave rushed down the hall to find Kozak. He had serious questions. He finally spotted Kozak leaving the building.

Dave hurried toward him, but a group of reporters were in the way. Cameras, lights, and microphones surrounded him. "Dave, will these revelations discredit Forrester?"

"Not now, guys," Dave said. "Dr. Kozak!"

He tried to get past. But the crowd pressed in closer. Rapid-fire questions filled the air.

"Rowrrrrr!" Dave roared. He lunged forward, jaws snapping at the reporters. A flashbulb went off. Dave didn't care. He raced after Kozak. But it was too late—Kozak was gone.

Just then, Lori appeared. "You know, that parent-teacher conference is in eight minutes."

Hollister caught up to them. "Dave, what on earth is wrong with you? You just barked at the reporters."

"It's the food poisoning. Gotta go. We'll talk later," he promised.

"What kind of food poisoning makes you bark like a dog?" Hollister pressed Dave.

"Gotta go!" Dave called as he ran down the hall.

Lori and Hollister looked at one another. "Parent-teacher conference," she explained. "He's a *very* involved dad."

CHAPTER

Dave had to find out more about the animal experiments at Kozak's lab. But he was already in the doghouse at home. If he missed that parent-teacher conference again, who knew what Rebecca would do?

"So sorry." Dave apologized to Rebecca and the teacher when he finally reached the school. "I just got out of court."

"No problem." The teacher pointed to a sandwich on her desk. "I hope you don't mind. I'm squeezing you in at lunch, so—"

"Ooh, yeah." Dave stared at the sandwich. "You go right ahead." His mouth watered, and he sniffed the air. The sandwich smelled delicious.

"What is that?" he asked. "Turkey with garlic, mayo, American cheese, Belgian endive on wheat and sunflower-seed bread?"

"Yes, it is," the teacher said, surprised.

Rebecca looked at her husband. How had he known all of that?

"We order in from the same place at work," Dave explained.

"I made this at home," the teacher said.

Dave couldn't stop staring at the sandwich.

"Do you want half?" the teacher asked.

Rebecca glared at her husband.

He tore his gaze away from the sandwich. "So about Josh?" Dave said.

"Well, up until a month ago, he was one of my best math students. And then suddenly . . ." She signaled a plunge in grades with her hand. "And we're just sort of . . . searching for an explanation."

Rebecca looked at Dave.

Then the teacher bit into her sandwich.

Dave whimpered. He wanted that sandwich so much!

Rebecca shot him an angry look. Typical Dave, she thought. She turned to the teacher apologetically. "You know I think the problem—"

Dave knew he had to get control. He was here for Josh. He was a man, not a dog! He gathered his strength. "Honey, if I could," he interrupted as he put his hand over Rebecca's and smiled at her. "I think the problem is me. I've been very pre—"

Dave stopped talking. Outside the window, a cat climbed a tree. *Cat!* His brain raced. His muscles tightened. He sat straight up.

"—pre . . . pre . . . preoccupied . . ." Dave clamped his mouth shut. The cat was playing in the tree, practically taunting Dave.

The teacher and Rebecca looked at Dave, waiting for him to finish.

Rebecca was getting annoyed. ". . . with?" she prompted.

Dave heard Rebecca. But her voice sounded far away. The cat was all he could think about. But this meeting was important. He had to focus.

". . . with work lately, and it's taken a toll—on everybody." He squeezed his wife's hand. "But especially the kids. I only just realized this in the last day or so. But I want you to rest assured . . . I'm going to do everything I can from here on in to be there for Josh. And I'm sure we'll get these grades turned around in a hurry. He's a great kid."

Dave was quivering now, trying to concentrate.

The teacher smiled at Dave. She thought his trembling meant he cared. "He is. He really is."

Rebecca was touched, too. She reached for Dave's hand. It was moments like this that made her remember why she had married him.

Dave jumped up. "Gotta get back to court," he said hurriedly. "Itwaswonderfultomeetyou.Honey

Iloveyouseeyoutonight." His words ran together. He was already out the door.

Rebecca looked at the teacher. "He's in the middle of a big case."

"I completely understand—I've been watching it on the news! He seems like a great dad!"

"Yeah," said Rebecca. "He is."

Outside, Dave chased the cat across the schoolyard. He followed into the street, skirting cars and trucks. An animal control truck slammed on its breaks and barely missed them.

Dave's neighbor Baxter was driving his Porsche on the same street, talking on the cell phone as his dog Attila watched from the passenger seat. Dave and the cat darted in front of the car. Baxter hit the brakes and yelled as a garbage truck crashed into them.

Dave paused and followed the cat into an alley. His heart pounded, loud and quick. *Thump-thump-thump. Thump-thump-thump.*

"Rrrr," he growled. The cat slipped under a

Dumpster. "I gotcha now!" Dave cried.

He reached under the Dumpster, searching. But he was searching with paws, not hands. Oh, no! He'd turned into a dog again! "Aw, nuts!" Upset, he rolled onto his back. "What I wouldn't give just to have rabies," he said with a moan.

The cat saw its chance for escape. In a flash, it ducked around Dave. Once the cat was safely out of reach, it turned and hissed.

"Give it a rest, will you?" Dave asked.

Suddenly, a loop of rope fell over the cat. Someone from animal control had gotten it.

"Ha! Serves you right," Dave said. But then, a second loop fell over him. "This is just not my week."

Back at Grant and Strictland, Larry and Gwen were busy running tests. Larry had found Khyi-yag-po at the animal shelter and brought him back to the lab. Now they were examining a rabbit. Kozak watched. So did Khyi-yag-po, the rats, the snake, and all the other animals.

"I think we've got it. This one got the serum two days ago," Gwen said, pointing to the rabbit. "So far, cell degeneration has ceased with no side effects."

"You're sure?" Kozak asked. "You're absolutely sure?"

"I'm sure," Gwen replied.

"I've done it!" Kozak cried, laughing.

"Yes, we have," Gwen said.

"I'll call Strictland. He'll want an injection right away!" Kozak said excitedly.

"Can we do that?" asked Larry. "Isn't there, like, an FDA?"

Kozak shook his head. "The man's got one lung and somebody else's kidney. He'll risk it." Kozak turned to leave, then glanced back at Khyi-yag-po. "Make as much serum as you can manufacture. And don't worry—it works. And we are all about to be very, very wealthy."

The animals looked at each other. They were in real trouble now.

CHAPTER

10

At the animal shelter, a worker walked Dave to a row of cages. "We're full up today, so you be a good boy and share your cage, okay?" He stopped in front of a cage with a poodle inside.

"Kinda cramped, don't you think?" Dave barked.

"Other way, pal," the guy said and put Dave in a cage with a very large English mastiff.

"Any chance I could get in with the poodle instead?" Dave asked.

The worker locked the cage.

"Wait, come back. I'm allergic to dogs," Dave

barked. He turned to the mastiff. "Look, pal. I've had a really bad week, okay? So don't give me any beef, or I will kick your mastiff tail right across this cage. We clear on that?"

The mastiff growled at Dave, baring its fangs.

Dave shrank back. "Okay, all good. I'm taking a nap," he told the mastiff. He tried to sound tough. "Don't wake me unless I'm human."

Dave closed his eyes. When he opened them later, the mastiff was stretched out over him. Dave felt like a mattress. Even worse, he was still a dog.

Then the door opened. "That's him!" a familiar voice exclaimed.

"Kids!" Dave barked.

"I knew Dad brought you back here," Carly said. "The jerk!"

"Hey!" Dave protested with a bark.

The worker let Dave out, and Carly and Josh hugged him as Trey looked on.

"Where'd you go?" Josh asked. "We've been looking all over for you."

"I was trying to work. Then I turned into a dog again. Wasn't much to do after that but come here," Dave barked.

Trey scratched Shaggy's head. "Hello, Trey." Dave wagged his tail. "Hey! Why is my tail wagging? I don't like you . . . do I?"

Then Dave turned to Josh. "And what's with the uniform?" he asked.

A little while later, Carly and Trey dropped Josh and Shaggy at the football field. "There's a game today? I thought you said they hadn't started yet." Dave barked to Josh.

"Be good, okay, buddy?" Josh said as he tied Dave to a bench and ran to join his team.

"I'm excited to see you play!" Dave barked.

By the middle of the last quarter, Josh's team was way ahead. The score: forty-four to seven. But Josh hadn't played at all. He wasn't even paying attention. He was sitting on the bench, reading lines from *Grease*.

Dave paced back and forth. "Why haven't you

gotten in? This is an outrage. When I turn human again, I'm making some phone calls!"

"Douglas!" The coach strode up to Josh. "You're in at tailback!"

The other players groaned and rolled their eyes.

"It's okay, coach," Josh said quickly. "You don't have to play me."

"What?" Dave barked, shocked. How could his son not want to play?

"Everybody plays," the coach said. "Come on."

Josh didn't move. "But with the game on the line and all . . ."

"Douglas!" yelled the coach. "We're up by thirty points. Get in there!" Slowly, Josh strapped on his helmet. He shuffled onto the field.

"C'mon, Josh!" Dave barked. "Show 'em what you can do!"

The players took their positions. "No, Douglas!" the coach shouted. "Further back."

Josh moved.

"That's too far!" the coach yelled.

Josh moved again.

"Stop! There!" the coach cried.

Seconds later, the center snapped the ball to the quarterback. The quarterback turned to hand the ball to Josh.

Josh tripped over his feet and fell against the quarterback. The quarterback grunted. Then he forced the ball into Josh's hands.

Josh froze. He looked around frantically. He didn't know where to go. Finally, he started down the field.

Crash! Three players from the other team plowed into him. The ball flew into the air.

An opposing player grabbed it, turned, and ran for a touchdown.

"Oooh!" Dave howled sadly. "That was . . . ooh."

Josh trudged back to the bench. Dave trotted over and put his head on his son's knee. "Don't worry, pal," Dave tried to tell him. "You'll get 'em next time!"

Josh sighed. "Thanks, pal."

"I don't get it." Dave shook his furry head. "I thought you loved football."

After the game, Dave followed Josh home. "Wish I could buy you an ice cream," Dave barked.

Just then, Tracy, Josh's friend, appeared. She eyed Josh's uniform.

"*Football!*" she screeched. "That's why you're not trying out?" She stamped her feet. "You hate football!"

Dave reared back. "What?"

"Shhh!" Josh looked around nervously. "I know! But my dad loves it."

"So what?" Tracy said.

"So, all he cares about is having a son who's a good football player. You should hear him." Josh mimicked his father, "'You'll be just like your old man!' If I told him I wanted to do a musical instead, he'd, like, write me off as a son!"

"Josh!" Dave yipped, surprised. "That's not true! I didn't want you to . . . I just thought . . . I don't know what I thought." He hung his head.

"Josh, is your father a stupid man?" Tracy asked.

"No," Josh answered. "But he is clueless. Which in some ways is better."

"Even so. Eventually he's going to realize you stink," Tracy said, "and you hate it."

Josh shook his head. "Not if he makes me quit before he sees a game."

Tracy and Dave both looked at Josh, confused.

"He told me I can only play if I keep my grades up. So I started flunking math—"

Dave's ears stood straight up. He gasped. That's why Josh was failing! he realized.

"But he just let me off with a warning," Josh went on. "So now I gotta flunk English. And maybe history. And home ec, which is really hard to fail."

"*Noooooooo!*" Dave howled sadly.

"You'd rather wreck your future than tell your dad you hate football?" Tracy asked.

Soon they walked by Baxter's house, where the ruined Porsche was attached to a tow truck. Josh looked at the Porsche, then back at Tracy. "I can get the grades back up! As long as he makes me quit in time. So really, it's more like I'm playing chicken with my future."

Josh would rather flunk three subjects than tell me he doesn't want to play football? Dave slumped to the ground. "How did I let this happen?" he asked himself. "Am I that bad a father?"

A little while later, Carly was busy printing out Animal Rescue Group pamphlets in her room. Trey sat on the bed, reading one.

"So what do you think of the new pamphlet?" Carly asked.

"It's infuriating. I mean, in a good way. It makes me want to do something about animal testing. You rock!" Trey complimented Carly.

Carly smiled and leaned over to kiss him.

"What's going on here?" Dave barked as he walked into the room. He leaped onto the bed between the two teenagers. "And what's this?" He nosed around the pamphlets for a minute. "This is really well done. Carly, you did this?"

"And admit it," Trey said. "This is so much more effective than a tattoo."

"That's what I said," Dave barked.

"Ugh," Carly said to her boyfriend. "You sound like my dad."

"Well, he's got a point," Trey countered.

"I can't believe you're taking his side," Carly protested.

"Trey, you are my new favorite boyfriend," Dave yipped.

"Think about it," Trey continued. "Do you really want an ARG tattoo after that testimony? Snakes with dog tails? He made the whole movement look ridiculous."

Carly frowned. "One thing I learned from Forrester is that just because something seems ridiculous doesn't mean it's wrong. It just takes more courage to stand up for it."

"Wow. I was so wrong." Dave gazed up at Carly. "You're really committed to this, aren't you?

Sweetheart, I'm so proud of you." He licked her face.

Carly giggled. "I mean, just imagine what would have happened to Shaggy if we hadn't stolen him from Grant and Strictland."

Dave caught his breath. "You *what*!" They had found the real Shaggy in the laboratory? That changes everything! Dave thought. Maybe the sheepdog had been part of an experiment! Maybe that's why I keep turning into a dog.

Trey leaned closer to Carly. Then he eyed Dave. He picked up a chew toy. "Go fetch, boy!"

"I am not your boy, and I am not going any-where until I—" Dave barked.

Trey tossed the toy.

Dave couldn't help himself—he had to run after it. "I'll be right back." He bounded out of the room and the door slammed shut. "Ugh, I have got to stop doing that."

Just then Josh showed up, singing a song from *Grease*.

"What?" Josh stopped singing. "Why are you looking at me like that?"

Dave barked. "You're pretty good at that!" he asked Shaggy.

Not understanding, Josh brushed past him. "Hey!" he shouted to Carly and Trey, "let's order some pizza. Mom and Dad are out to dinner."

Oh, no! Dinner! Dave thought. Their anniversary! Rebecca was waiting for him at the restaurant!

At their favorite restaurant, Rebecca sat at a table for two by a large bay window. The seat across from her was empty, and it was dark and rainy outside.

"You should bring a book." a woman at the next table said. "The single woman's best friend."

"I'm not single," Rebecca said. "Yet."

Dave scurried down the street with a bouquet of roses in his mouth. "I'm late," he panted. "I'm late. I'm late."

Finally, he reached the restaurant and looked

in the window at his wife. He really wanted to be in there with her. "I'm late," he repeated. "And I'm also a dog."

He gazed sadly at his wife. "I'm sorry, honey."

"Shaggy!" Rebecca cried, spotting him.

She left the restaurant, then led Dave into the car. Uh-oh, he thought. She looks really mad.

Rebecca picked up her cell phone and called Dave at his office. "I cannot believe this," she said, leaving a message. "First you completely ignore me, and now you send a *dog* with roses in his mouth. Are you trying to push me away?"

"Uh-oh," Dave barked. "Shouldn't have brought the roses."

"We need to talk," Rebecca continued. "But I don't know how we're going to get past this one. I don't . . . Good-bye."

"No, honey!" Dave barked.

She looked at Dave the dog tearfully. Then she began to drive. "It wasn't always like this, Shaggy. He used to be there for everything. And if he couldn't be? He'd send flowers. And leave notes. With these silly little rhymes . . ." She trailed off, unable to speak.

Dave whimpered. "Honey, no. Don't cry!"

"Shaggy, don't you cry!" Rebecca stopped at a light and hugged him. "Is this how it ends? With him who-knows-where and me hugging the dog?"

"No, Reb, I'm going to figure out what happened to me," Dave promised. "I'm going to fix it. I'll be a better man, I promise." He raised his head to look into Rebecca's eyes. "I love you."

Rebecca heard Shaggy bark, "Rar ruv roo!" She stared at him for a long moment, trying to figure out what he meant. "Don't go to the bathroom in the car," she finally told Dave. "We're almost home. Okay?"

Dave whined in frustration. Rebecca moved him off her lap and began to drive again. Dave turned to his wife. "Could you roll down the window so I can stick my head out?" he barked as they drove home.

CHAPTER

That night, Dave slept in the garage again. When he woke up, it was 3:00 A.M.—and he was human. Dave snapped his fingers. He knew what he had to do.

A little while later, he'd left a note for Rebecca and was ringing the doorbell to his boss's house. Hollister swung open the door, glaring. "Dave, it's three in the morning. And you want a warrant to search the Grant and Strictland laboratory? They're the victims!"

"Ken, you've got to trust me on this one," Dave

pleaded. "Kozak's hiding something. I've got a hunch Forrester was framed for the arson, after all."

"If Forrester was framed, why's he throwing in the towel?" Hollister asked.

"What are you talking about?" Dave stepped back.

"He's pleading out," Hollister replied.

"Why wasn't I told?" Dave said.

"Because you're off the case," Hollister explained.

Dave was shocked. "What? How could you?"

Hollister held up a copy of yesterday's newspaper with a photo of Dave growling. "Hey, I've got people to answer to. And so when they call me, and say, 'So, Ken, why the heck is your deputy barking at reporters?' I don't really have a good response." He paused. "The jury convenes at ten to hear Forrester's plea. I'll handle it myself. I want you to either get your head screwed on straight or find another job. Is that clear?"

Dave took a deep breath. If Hollister didn't

believe him, no one else would either. He was on his own. "Yes, sir," he said, and stalked off.

It was still the dead of night. Dave parked in the Grant and Strictland lot and switched the engine off. Silence filled the air. He turned off the headlights, and darkness settled around him. It was time to investigate.

Dave moved quickly around the building. He sniffed each part of the wall. Finally, he came to an air vent. His nose twitched. He stopped. The vent led somewhere. . . .

He knelt beside it. From deep within the building, Khyi-yag-po raised his head. He felt sick and tired because of all those tests. But he sensed Dave was somewhere near and needed guidance.

"Arf! Arf!" he barked. The rabbits and monkey joined in. "Roof, roooof!" They barked as loud as they could.

Dave strained to listen. What was that noise? Faint arfs and woofs were traveling through the air ducts and out through the vent. Shaggy and the animals! They were telling him where to go!

Carefully, Dave removed the grating. He tried to climb inside. "Ugh!" he grunted. He was too big. How could he ever fit inside? There was only one way. He had to become a dog. But could he make himself do it?

Dave stuck out his tongue. He panted like crazy. Faster and faster. His heart quickened. But it wasn't quite working. Finally, he found a stick and spotted someone nearby.

He ran over to the man. "Hey, buddy. Will you throw this stick, like, as far as you can over there?"

The man eyed Dave warily.

"Come on, it'll just take a second," Dave begged.

The man threw the stick. Dave ran on all fours, picked the stick up with his teeth and brought it back to the man. Was this going to help turn him into a dog? Dave wondered.

"Do it again," Dave said.

"Five bucks," the man replied.

Dave pulled out his wallet.

"Ten," the man tried.

Dave held out a ten-dollar bill.

The man took the money and got ready to throw the stick. "Speed or distance?" he asked.

"Distance," Dave said.

The man threw the stick as hard as he could.

Dave ran after it on all fours, his heart beating quickly. The stick bounced on the ground, and when Dave picked it up he was a shaggy sheepdog! "Wow, I can't believe that worked!" he exclaimed as he ran toward the air vent.

The man who had thrown the stick stared incredulously. Had a human being just turned into a dog?

When Dave started crawling through the ducts, the animals stopped barking. Kozak, Strictland, Gwen, and Larry had returned to the lab. Strictland sat in his wheelchair and eyed Khyi-yag-po.

"And to think, I was never a dog person," he said. Then he began to cough.

Kozak held a needle, ready to inject the serum. "Need a minute?" he asked.

"I'm not sure I have a minute," Strictland replied.

Gwen rolled up Strictland's sleeve.

"The transistor, the microchip, the artificial heart. They'll be footnotes compared to this," Kozak said as he plunged the needle into Strictland's arm.

Directly above them, in the air duct, Dave could hear everything. Khyi-yag-po peered up, and their eyes met.

Then they both watched Strictland. The old man flexed his arms. He began to pull himself out of the wheelchair.

The serum was working! Gwen and Larry leaned closer, growing excited.

Suddenly, Strictland fell back in his chair. His spine stiffened. His arms curled oddly. He was paralyzed—hands stuck out like paws, tongue hanging out like a dog.

"He's going into shock!" Gwen cried. "The serum doesn't work!"

"Of course it works," Kozak said calmly. "I just didn't give it to him."

Gwen and Larry stared at Kozak.

He leaned over Strictland. "Sorry to do this to you, Lance," he said, not sounding sorry at all. "But I couldn't let you take all the credit again. This isn't going to be like the baldness cream. In so many ways."

"Is he . . . dead?" asked Gwen.

"No. He's fully conscious, but unable to move or speak. The doctors will think it's dementia. They'll probably put him in an institution, depending on his health plan. The drug will wear off in a few months. But by then, I'll be CEO. And unimaginably wealthy."

"This wasn't part of the deal—" Larry said.

"I'll cut you in on his share," Kozak said.

"But I'm cool with it," Larry replied.

"Fine by me," Gwen agreed.

"Good. Wheel him up to his office. Park him at his desk. Or perhaps I should say *my* desk."

Kozak swung his head back and laughed. He opened his mouth wide. Above him, Dave peered down and a glob of saliva fell from his tongue. It dropped down . . . down . . . straight into Kozak's mouth.

"Yech!" Kozak cried. Inside Kozak's body, his cells started to transform immediately, just like Dave's had. They grew tails and chased each other around.

He looked up and spied Dave in the air duct.

"Uh-oh," Dave said. He turned and ran back the way he had come.

"What was that?" Gwen asked.

But Kozak just ran for the elevator.

In seconds, Kozak found the broken-off grate. A security camera was pointing right at it.

"Let's check the video," Kozak said as they headed inside.

CHAPTER

12

At the Douglas home, Rebecca had just spotted Dave's note.

"'I'll explain everything soon!'" she read out loud.

Rebecca sat up, confused. Where was Dave? What was going on? Then she saw the foot of the bed. I LOVE YOU was spelled out in rose petals. Smiling, she sprang out of bed.

Outside, Baxter opened his door to let Attila out and gasped. None of his rosebushes had any petals left.

Back at Grant and Strictland, Kozak and Larry were watching the security video.

"Holy cow!" Larry cried as they watched a video of Dave turning into a dog. "*Holy cow!* Do you realize the significance of what we just saw?" Larry asked.

Kozak ejected the tape and smashed it. "Yes, if word of it gets out, we'll be ruined. Okay, okay. Here's what you're going to do. . . ."

Dave was running up his street, panting.

Inside his house, Carly was sitting at the bottom of the stairs when Josh came down. Rebecca had already left.

"Where's Trey?" Hosh asked. "We're going to be late for school! I should've gotten a ride from Mom." He paused, noticing his sister looked really upset. "What's the matter?"

"Do you realize what's happening?" she asked Josh. "Mom and Dad are splitting up."

"How do you know?" Josh said.

"Come on, Josh. It's obvious," Carly replied.

Scratch, scratch. Dave the dog was pawing at the door.

Josh opened the door. "Shaggy!" he exclaimed.

"Where have you been?" Carly asked.

"I just witnessed a crime and an innocent man's about to go to jail!" Dave barked wildly. "Why do you guys look so sad?"

Carly turned back to Josh. "Did you see that note he left? 'I'll explain everything.' We're going to get the talk, Josh."

"What talk?" Josh asked.

"The Mom and Dad are having problems talk. Then Dad will move out. They'll say it's temporary. But it won't be."

Dave stopped suddenly. They thought he and Rebecca were getting a divorce! "Carly, that's not it at all."

"You sure?" Josh asked.

"He didn't even come home last night,"

Carly continued. "But if you ask me, he stopped caring a long time before that."

"No, no, no!" Dave cried. Quickly, he bounded to the living room. Scrabble was on the top shelf. He needed that game to tell his kids what was going on.

He jumped onto the couch. Using it as a springboard, he leaped onto the back of the armchair. From there, he vaulted toward the shelves. He stretched as far as he could, knocking the Scrabble box with his nose.

Crash! Dave and the game hit the floor. Tiles flew everywhere. He had to work quickly now.

Josh and Carly rushed in. "Shaggy!" Carly was annoyed. "Will you stop making a—"

She gasped. Josh's eyes widened. Shaggy sat panting in front of a line of letters. They read, I AM DAD.

"Finally!" Dave barked.

"That's impossible," Carly said slowly.

"No, it isn't," Dave barked and shook his head.

"How?" Josh asked.

Dave nosed more tiles around. This time he spelled GRANT AND STRICTLAND.

"Grant and Strictland?" Josh asked.

"Forrester says they created mutant animals," Carly realized. "And that's where I found Shaggy. And Shaggy bit Dad." She sucked in her breath. "Oh, Daddy!"

She wrapped her arms around Dave and hugged him tightly. "I did this. It's all my fault. I'm so sorry. . . ."

"It's okay, sweetheart." Dave licked her face.

"Can you ever forgive me?" she asked.

Dave nodded. "I already did, kiddo," he barked.

Carly hugged him again. "We gotta call Mom!" She ran off. Josh and Dave were alone. "So," Josh began, "you saw the game yesterday?"

Again, Dave nodded.

"I'm sorry. I didn't want to let you down," Josh said sheepishly. "But I'm just no good."

Dave barked. "Josh! You are good! Just not at

that! Where'd that book go?" He hurried into the kitchen, and found the script for *Grease*. He grabbed it with his teeth and carried it to Josh. "Do this," he told his son. "Not football. Okay?"

"Thanks, Dad."

Then Dave pushed a math book at Josh, too. "And quit flunking math!"

Josh figured out what his dad was trying to tell him and grinned. "It's a deal."

All at once, Dave's ears shot up. He'd heard a noise outside. A noise he didn't like.

"What's the matter?" Josh asked.

"Someone's peeing on my lawn!" Dave yelled. He raced out the door. Attila, who wore a neck brace and bandages, was lifting his leg by the shrubs in Dave's backyard, again!

"Nobody makes on my lawn and gets away with it! I'm going to—ohhh!"

Dave fell to one side, then looked up. Gwen and Larry were standing over him. Gwen held the cattle prod.

"Hello there, Mr. Douglas," Larry said. Gwen poked him with the cattle prod again. Dave could barely move.

In a flash, Gwen and Larry tossed Dave into the back of their car.

"Dad!" Josh cried as he and Carly dashed out the front door.

"Hit it," Larry yelled to Gwen.

Gwen floored the gas, leaving Carly and Josh in the dust.

"Daddy! Dad!" Carly and Josh yelled.

Dave felt helpless. "Don't worry, kids," he tried to say. "I'll be okay. I think. . . ."

Dave stared out of a cage. He was in the Grant and Strictland laboratory with all the other animals. Kozak was staring at him.

"I'm very sorry you're a dog. I am. Also very sorry you won't be leaving here alive. People will wonder where you disappeared to, but then dogs do wander off," Kozak told Dave.

"You'll never get away with this, Kozak," Dave barked.

Kozak's sharp teeth glistened under the harsh lights. "Before you die, though, we'd like to run some tests and try to figure out just how the heck *you* turned into *him*."

Kozak stuck his finger in the cage to point at Dave. "I can't wait to get inside that body of yours and poke around—*oww*!" Dave snapped his jaws shut—right on Kozak's finger.

"You filthy little mongrel!" Kozak jumped back. "That was not nice. We're going to work on that attitude when I get back. Right now, we have to run upstairs. It seems Dr. Strictland's had some sort of health crisis. And of course after that," he paused to scratch his ear, "I'll be off to court to watch Justin Forrester—" He scratched even faster. "—back down to save his skin. See you soon." Still scratching, Kozak headed for the elevator.

Finally, Dave could get some answers. "Who are you, anyway?" he asked Khyi-yag-po.

"R-r-r-ooof!" the sheepdog barked.

"Really? All the way from Tibet? So let me ask this." Dave paused. "Why did you bite me?"

Again, the sheepdog barked.

"How can I help you if I'm a dog?" Dave barked back.

Khyi-yag-po barked an apology.

"No kidding you didn't think about that!"

"Arf, arf!" This time, the monkey barked, suggesting Dave turn human.

"If I knew how to do that, don't you think I would? It happens when I sleep. But there's no time for that. Got to be another way!"

Khyi-yag-po barked.

"Turning into a dog? I just . . . act like a dog. I think . . . I mean, I run around, or get agitated, and my heart starts pounding in my ears. . . . My heart—maybe that's it! Got to get my heart rate down. Deep breaths, deep breaths. I'm on a beach, surrounded by fire hydrants, food everywhere. Pounds and pounds of raw chuck.

And mailmen, very slow mailmen."

Nothing happened. "Boy!" Dave shook his head. "It's tough to get calm when you're locked in a cage."

Khyi-yag-po barked. He sat in the deep-thinking pose he knew from the monastery.

He wanted Dave to copy him. "Meditation? It's worth a shot," Dave said. He crossed his dog legs as best he could. The other animals did, too.

"Woof! Arf!" The sheepdog barked directions.

"Inhale," Dave said repeateding Khyi-yag-po's instructions. He took a deep breath. "Exhale." He let it out. Again and again.

Khyi-yag-po howled a chant. "Arooooo."

"Arooooooo!" repeated Dave. *Thump, thump* went his heart. *Thump . . . thump . . .* It slowed down.

Outside, Trey pulled up to Carly's house. "Sorry, I'm late," he said.

"Get in and drive!" Carly ordered.

"What's the matter with—" he began.

"Our dad's been dognapped!" Carly said.

Trey stared at her, confused.

"Just drive!" she cried.

Back at the lab, Dave was still chanting. Suddenly, he was human again! And way too big for the cage. Dave's legs were bent uncomfortably and his face was squashed against the wire. "Okay, new problem."

"Arf!" barked Khyi-yag-po.

Dave twisted around. A key ring hung on the wall, next to the cattle prod. "I see it. I just have to get to it."

He rocked back and forth in the cage. The cage lurched forward, closer to the key.

Dave swayed harder. The cage tipped over. "This is bad," Dave said as the cage hit the floor.

"Ahh, bad idea. Bad Dave!" he cried, upside down and stuck in place.

Dave eyed the other animals. "Okay, who's got a plan?"

CHAPTER 13

Meanwhile, Josh, Carly, and Trey were driving to the lab. Carly and Josh had told Trey what had happened to their father.

"Okay, assuming that's all true—how do we save him?" Trey asked.

"We need a plan," Carly said.

Meanwhile, inside the laboratory, *all* the animals were jumping around, trying to push the snake's cage off the shelf so it could escape.

"One, two, three, jump!" Dave directed. Cages thumped and rattled. "Now the rabbits! Ready, jump!" Up on the shelf, the bunny cage lurched forward, knocking into the snake's. The snake's cage moved further off the edge.

"We're close now. Monkey, give me one more to the right. Hold on tight, snake. Ready? Jump!"

The monkey leaped. His cage rammed into the snake's. It's cage skittered. It teetered . . . it tottered . . . and then *crash*! It hit the floor and the top popped off.

The snake slithered free.

"Now," said Dave, "get Khiag-Lo." He turned to the sheepdog. "Am I pronouncing that correctly?"

"Arf!"

"Khyi-yag-po. Sorry. Whatever happened to 'Rover'?" Dave replied.

The snake slid to the sheepdog's cage. Then the snake uncurled, stretching up toward the latch and pushed it up with the tip of its head. The latch slipped open.

Khyi-yag-po stepped out of the cage.

"Now the cart!" ordered Dave.

The sheepdog trotted over to the cart. He pushed it against the wall, underneath the keys.

Then the snake wound himself up the cart's leg, to the top. He pushed against the key ring.

The keys toppled off the hook and clattered to the floor. "Woof! Arf!" The rabbits barked excitedly. The monkey clapped.

"Way to go!" Dave cried.

Khyi-yag-po took the keys in his mouth and padded over to Dave. Dave grabbed the keys and opened the lock.

"Excellent work, everybody!" He realized he needed some clothes. "Could someone hand me a lab coat?"

The sheepdog tossed Dave a lab coat. "Thanks, fantastic job." He patted Khyi-yag-po on the head. He reached out to pet the cobra, but couldn't quite do it. "You did great. Let's get out of here!" he said.

One by one, he helped the animals into the air duct. "Remember," he called to Khyi-yag-po, leading the way, "left, left, right. Then just follow the daylight."

Now it was Dave's turn. He was too big to fit in the duct. He'd just have to make a run for it. "Okay, I'll meet you outside," he called. He started for the door.

Zzzzzap! Dave's body stiffened and paralyzed, he hit the floor. "Ooof."

He looked up. Gwen was standing over him with the cattle prod.

The monkey and rabbits realized Dave was in trouble. They barked to the sheepdog to stop. But it was too late. Khyi-yag-po was already outside.

Josh, Carly, and Trey were just pulling into the parking lot. "This way!" they shouted. "Over here!"

The sheepdog leaped into the backseat. Trey slammed the door. The car squealed away.

"Woof!" Khyi-yag-po barked in panic. They couldn't leave. They needed to wait for Dave and the other animals! "Woof!" He pawed the window desperately.

"We won't let them get away with it," Carly said, not understanding. "Don't worry, Daddy."

"Arf?" the sheepdog barked. No one realized that it was Khyi-yag-po in the car, not Dave!

At the lab, Gwen and Larry squeezed Dave back into the cage. They set up machines, getting the lab ready to do some tests on Dave.

"You seem like good kids with a bright future ahead of you." Dave said. "How can you do this? Kidnapping an innocent man? Locking him in a cage?"

Gwen and Larry ignored Dave and prepared the virus injection machine. "We are crossing a line here, Gwen. You know that, right?" Larry said.

"We crossed that line a long time ago," Gwen replied. "Deal with it."

"Yeah, yeah, I guess so," Larry said.

Gwen attached the last wire to the machine. They were ready. Gwen picked up the cattle prod as Larry unlocked Dave's cage.

Behind the assistants, the snake uncoiled from the vent and hung straight down from the ceiling. Quietly, the monkey shimmied down the snake's body. Gwen and Larry didn't see a thing.

"You can't get away with this," Dave said. "You know that, right?"

"Now," she told Dave. "Be a good little schnauzer, and do just what we say. . . ."

Zzzzzap! Bzzzzz! The monkey had grabbed the cattle prod and zapped Gwen and Larry! They both slumped to the floor. The monkey raised his arms in triumph.

"Nice job, monkey!" Dave exclaimed.

In the car, Khyi-yag-po was barking wildly.

Carly turned. "Please don't be mad, Daddy!"

"Don't worry," Josh said. "We're going to take you to Mom and explain everything."

"*Baraoooooo!*" Khyi-yag-po howled.

Carly turned around. "He's really angry," she said to Trey.

"Wouldn't you be?" Trey replied.

Back inside Grant and Strictland, Dave was able to move again. So he pushed himself out of the cage and bundled Gwen and Larry into two other cages.

"We have to go," Dave told them. "But don't worry. We'll be back with policemen!"

The animals jumped onto the cart. The monkey barked menacingly, squeezing the cattle prod for effect.

"I think maybe I should hold the cattle prod now," Dave said.

The monkey handed it over.

Dave covered the cart with a blanket and wheeled it onto the elevator, and then through the lobby. He walked slowly, without a care in the world, like a good employee. When he reached the front entrance, he peered behind him. All clear. He looked in front of him. All clear. Then he broke into a run.

CHAPTER 14

Rebecca was at her office, looking at a blueprint with a coworker. "I'd rather see a bigger atrium—"

Just then, Carly, Josh, and Trey burst in. "Mom! We need to talk!" Carly cried.

Rebecca looked up, surprised. "Could you give me a minute?" she said to her coworker.

"Oh, sure," the coworker replied.

"Why aren't you in school? And why is the dog here?" Rebecca asked.

"It's not a dog!" Carly exclaimed. "It's Dad!"

"I thought we were going to break it to her slowly," Josh said.

Carly ignored him. "Grant and Strictland's been running these crazy animal experiments. And somehow when Shaggy bit Dad, he turned him into a dog."

Rebecca looked at the sheepdog. Khyi-yag-po whimpered and covered his eyes.

"Carly, that's impossible," Rebecca said.

"No, it's true. It's . . ." Carly peered around the office. She had to prove this. Her eyes lit on the computer. That was it! "The computer! The other night, he was typing on the computer. C'mon, Dad. Type Mom a message!"

She pulled Khyi-yag-po over to Rebecca's desk. Reluctantly, he hopped on the chair. He stared at the computer, doing nothing.

"Come on!" said Josh. "You did it at home!"

"You know, like this." Carly put a pen in her mouth. She started to type, poking at keys with the pen. She held the pen out. "C'mon, Dad. Please?"

"Just one sentence! 'I am Dad.' How about just 'Dad'? How about just 'D'?"

Rebecca looked at the dog, then at Trey, who shrugged.

"Kids." Rebecca sighed. They were having such a tough time lately. Who could blame them for acting a little nutty? Maybe they wanted this dog to be their dad. That way he'd be home all the time. "I know these past couple of days have been very difficult. . . ."

The phone rang. "Hello?" Rebecca answered.

"Honey, it's me!" Dave was calling from his car. Three white rats were in the car with him. Their heads were sticking out the window, and their tongues were flapping in the wind. The rabbits sat in Dave's lap, and the monkey relaxed in the passenger seat. The snake had curled itself around the headrest.

Rebecca turned to her children. "It's your father."

Josh and Carly stared at the sheepdog, not believing it.

"Hi. Wow, so many questions. First off, do you know why the kids just showed up at my office with Shaggy?" Rebecca asked Dave.

"You mean Khyi-yag-po?"

"Khyi-yag-who?"

"'Po.' That's his real name. How'd the kids find him? That's weird. . . ."

"That's not the only thing that's weird. They've been trying to convince me that he's you."

Carly sank into a chair. Trey put a hand on her shoulder. Josh looked at them, confused by what was happening. How could they have misunderstood?

"He's not me—" Dave said.

"Yeah, I gathered that," she said.

"But they're half right," Dave told her. "Meet me at the courthouse as soon as possible, and I'll explain everything."

"I'd like you to explain it now."

In the car, the monkey was trying on sunglasses.

"Put those away!" Dave said. "I gotta go—the monkey's getting in the glove compartment. Meet me at the courthouse with a change of clothes." He started to hang up. "I love you!" he said.

"Dave, wait!" Rebecca said. But it was too late. He'd already hung up.

"He wants us to meet him at the courthouse with a change of clothes," she said to the kids.

Khyi-yag-po barked. They all looked at him, trying to figure out what was going on.

"I don't get it," Josh said.

"It just doesn't make sense. . . ." Carly trailed off, starting to cry.

"You know," Rebecca said, "two nights ago, your father tried to tell me he'd turned into a dog."

They all looked at one another. Then, together they said: "Let's go to the courthouse!"

CHAPTER 15

At the courthouse, the trial was about to resume.

"All rise for the honorable Judge Whitaker," the bailiff said.

Back in his car, Dave was still stuck in freeway traffic, along with the rats, the monkey, the bunnies, and the snake. Dave looked at his watch. It was three minutes to ten. The trial would start at ten o'clock sharp. He put the car in park. He had to get going. He turned to the monkey. "You're in charge. Keep the windows cracked."

He opened the door and raced at full speed, past all the stopped cars. He stuck out his tongue. He panted. His heart beat quicker and quicker. *Thump-thump, thump-thump, thump-thump.* He leaped onto a car roof. Then he jumped from car to car on all fours. His legs grew shorter. His body stooped. His fur blew in the breeze.

He had turned back into a sheepdog!

He raced faster and faster, getting out at the exit and bounding down the streets.

Meanwhile Rebecca, Josh, Carly, Trey, and Khyi-yag-po had arrived at the courthouse and were waiting on the steps.

"This is ridiculous," Rebecca said. "I have to get back to work."

Suddenly, Josh's eyes got bigger. He pointed at something on the street. "Wait, look!"

Dave raced up to them, and stopped. "Deep breaths," he said to himself. "Slow that heart down."

"Dad, is that you?" Carly asked.

Dave barked. "It's me, kiddo."

Rebecca shook her head in disbelief. "It can't be. He's a dog!"

Dave looked at her. "Would a dog say this—I love you. Rai ruv roo!"

Rebecca looked startled. "What did you say?"

"Rai ruv roo! Rai ruv roo!" Dave barked as loud as he could.

"Oh, honey," Rebecca said. She believed him! "I love you, too!"

Then she hugged him tight. Dave's paws went around her. Then they turned into hands. He was human again!

Rebecca jumped back. Everyone looked at Dave, stunned.

"Tell me about it," Dave said. "Weird, huh?" He hugged his wife.

"That was cool!" Josh said.

Trey turned to Khyi-yag-po. "Can you do that?"

The sheepdog shook his head.

Carly hugged Dave. "Daddy, I'm so sorry. . . ."

"No, I'm the one who's sorry, kiddo. And I'm going to make it up to you. But right now, I've got a trial to stop."

Inside the courtroom, the judge banged her gavel. She turned to Forrester's lawyer. "Counsel, I understand you'd like to enter a plea at this time?"

"Yes, Your Honor. In return for a promise of leniency by the court, my client would like to plead—"

Dave burst into the room, with his family close behind. "Hold everything!" he shouted.

Everyone spun around to face him.

"Forrester's telling the truth!" cried Dave. "Kozak set the fire to cover up an illegal genetic-testing program."

The room buzzed with excitement. Forrester grinned. Kozak leaped to his feet. "That's preposterous. This man is clinically insane!" Then he whispered to the man next to him, "Excuse me, heading out."

"Kozak, sit!" Dave ordered.

Kozak sat.

The judge glared at Dave. "Mr. Douglas, it's my understanding you're no longer on this case."

Dave stepped close to his boss. He whispered, "Ken, if you ever trusted me, please trust me now. I won't let you down."

"Your track record lately isn't exactly—"

"Just give me one more chance. You won't regret it. I promise."

Hollister looked at him for a long moment, deciding. "He's back on, Your Honor. And we'd like to . . ."

Still sitting, Kozak inched toward the door.

"Kozak, stay!" Dave commanded.

Kozak froze in place.

"We'd like to recall Dr. Kozak to the stand," continued Hollister.

CHAPTER

The courtroom buzzed with excitement, and the judge called for order. "Dr. Kozak, please retake the stand."

"What's going on?" Forrester asked.

"I have no idea," his lawyer said. "But I'm not going to stop it."

As Kozak passed Dave, they growled at each other and sniffed.

"Counsel," the judge told Dave, "you are on a very short leash. This court has lost its patience for ridiculous behavior."

Dave glanced at Carly, sitting in the back. "Your

Honor, just because something seems ridiculous doesn't mean it's wrong. It just takes a little more courage to believe it."

Carly beamed.

"Don't let your courage get itself thrown out of my courtroom," she said. She turned to Kozak. "And if you step out of line, I will throw your courage out of my courtroom. Dr. Kozak, I'll remind you you're still under oath."

Dave faced the jury. "Ladies and gentlemen. . . a lot of us want to live forever. We want to believe in the fountain of youth. But we sometimes forget that there is no point in living forever if you're not with the people you love. I forgot that, but I found it out again, thanks to man's best friend, a dog named Shaggy."

His family nodded and smiled.

"That's very nice," the judge said. "But would you please get to the point?"

Dave turned back to the witness stand. "Yes, Your Honor. Mr. Kozak, two days ago you set fire to your lab to frame Justin Forrester because you needed to hide the fact that you were doing illegal genetic testing for a fountain of youth drug. Weren't you, Mr. Kozak?"

"No!" Kozak responded.

"May I remind you, you're under oath." Dave countered. "Did you set the fire? And are you performing illegal tests on animals? C'mon, boy!"

"No!" Kozak roared.

Dave edged closer and snarled at Kozak. Kozak growled back.

"Yes, you did!"

"No, I didn't. Rrr! Rrrrr!" Kozak countered.

"Yes, you did! Rrrrr! Rrrrrrr!"

"Nnnnnnoooooo!" Kozak howled.

"No more growling," the judge said. "What are you, animals? Next person to growl goes to jail for contempt. I'm not playing. Get to your point or sit down."

Dave looked at Kozak, who was scratching his ear. "Tell the truth, you mutt!" Dave whispered.

"In the lab located in the basement of Grant and Strictland, are you holding and experimenting on monkeys that bark like dogs?" he asked in a voice that everyone could hear.

"No!" Kozak replied.

"Snakes with furry tails?" Dave asked.

Kozak scratched his ear furiously as he responded. "No!"

Forrester's lawyer stood. "Objection, Your Honor. My client's future—"

The judge banged her gavel. "Sustained. I've heard enough."

Dave looked at Kozak. His tongue was hanging out of his mouth. "Did you inject Mr. Strictland with a debilitating serum?"

"Gggggggrrrrrrrrrrr!" Kozak said.

The judge banged her gavel. "That's it, Mr. Douglas. You're through. Bailiff, please remove Mr. Douglas!"

"C'mon, you mutt!" Dave yelled at Kozak. "Tell us the truth!"

"Sit down now!" the judge thundered.

The bailiff, headed toward Dave and grabbed for him. Dave faked the bailiff out and grabbed his nightstick. "Kozak, fetch!" Dave called, tossing it across the room.

Kozak sprang out of his seat and bounded on all fours across the room. Then he grabbed the stick with his teeth. When he looked up, the entire courtroom was staring at him.

Kozak dropped the stick. He shrugged, as if running and fetching were no big deal. "Sorry," he said. "Been working long hours and sometimes the stress makes it . . ." Then he realized everyone was staring at his back. "What? What?" Kozak cried.

He twisted around to see what was going on. He had a long, shaggy tail! And it was wagging!. "AAAIIIEEEE!" he screamed.

Dave smiled at the judge. "Now if that's not evidence of genetic testing, I don't know what is."

The judge stared in disbelief. "On second

thought, bailiff," she said, "take *him* into custody."
She gestured at Kozak.

Forrester hugged his lawyer. He was free. He had been proven innocent.

The guard pulled Kozak toward the door. "For what?" Kozak asked. "Shuffling some DNA around? The animals don't care! They don't even understand what's happening to them. Don't you people realize I can make us all immortal?"

"Don't tell me animals don't understand," Dave said. "I know better."

"You haven't seen the last of me!" Kozak shouted at Dave. "You don't know who you're dealing with. I will have my revenge! Rrrrr! Rrrrr! Ooh!" he said to the bailiff excitedly. "Are we going outside?"

The trial was over. As everyone left the courtroom, Hollister and Dave stopped on the courthouse steps. "Buddy, I owe you an apology," Hollister said. "You got this one right, after all."

Hollister pointed to all the reporters and photographers. "And this is just the kind of exposure you need to get elected DA."

"Not right now, Ken," Dave said. "I've got more important people to talk to." He hurried over to his family.

"You did it! You're my hero!" Carly flung her arms around her father's neck.

"You don't know how good it is to hear that, kiddo," Dave said as he hugged her.

Dave kissed his wife. "So," he said, "what do you say we take that vacation to AWWW WAHH HOOO?"

Just then the lab animals dashed across the courthouse lawn, barking. "How did you guys get here?" Dave asked.

The monkey pointed across the grass. Dave's car, dented, steaming, and wrecked, was rammed against a stone post. Dave sighed. That was the last time he'd leave a monkey in the driver's seat!

CHAPTER

17

One week later, Dave was talking in a businesslike voice on his cell phone. "Ken, I'd love to take the case." He paused. "But I just don't have the time right now. I'm up to my neck here."

Dave was up to his neck, all right—but not with work. He was buried in sand on a beach in Hawaii. "I'll call you as soon as vacation's over. You, too. Bye."

Carly hung up the phone. Trey dumped a bucket of sand on Dave's chest. "Try getting out of that one," Carly said.

Dave struggled. But he couldn't get free. Then Rebecca came over. "Hug?" she asked Dave.

With a mighty effort, Dave shrugged off the sand. He stood up and hugged his wife. Then he kissed her.

She wrinkled her nose. "Eww, you're all gritty." She looked around. "Where's Khyi-yag-po?" she asked him.

"He said he was going for some exercise," Dave told her.

Trey pointed out to sea. "There he is!"

The shaggy sheepdog was surfing a big wave. He "hung ten" like an expert.

On the beach, people gasped. "Wow!" said Dave. "Three hundred years old, he can still ride the curl."

"Dad!" Josh called from down the beach. He held up a Frisbee. "Catch!"

"No, thanks," Dave said. "I'm not really in the mood—"

Josh threw the Frisbee.

"Got it!" Dave cried, taking off at a run, and catching it in his mouth.

Dog . . . human . . . whatever . . . who could resist a Frisbee?

Besides, did it really matter what he was? He was with his family, the people he loved more than anything else in the world. And that's what mattered most of all.